BY DANA D'ANGELO

The Knights Of Honor Trilogy
One True Knight
A Knight's Duty
Fallen Knight

Scottish Strife Series
The Highland Chief
The Highland Curse

Novellas
The Promise
Heart Of A Knight

D1173365

The Highland Chief

Scottish Strife Series
Book 1

Dana D'Angelo

Dedication

For Daryn R. Carrillo

Acknowledgment

As always, thanks to my husband for everything. Also my thanks go out to my friends and fans. I'm so grateful for your enthusiasm and support of my works. You're the ones that keep me writing!

Chapter 1

ন্ত্ৰ

England, 1560

What was that?

Darra Berchelaine's eyes opened abruptly. Rolling over to her side, she pushed herself to a seated position. Her hand rose to her chemise, clutching the material as she waited for the pounding in her chest to subside. She blinked a couple of times, her lungs expanding and contracting rapidly with each breath she took. Then slowly her breathing returned to normal. She dropped her hand onto the cool bed-clothes, and stared at the thick velvet curtain that surrounded her bed.

Straining her ears, she could detect the splattering of rain on the shutters, the noise like hard pebbles scattering across wooden panels. And just beyond the castle walls, she heard thunder rumbling, the reverberation rolling into her chamber, making it feel small and claustrophobic.

She licked her dry lips, wishing that she had some ale to quench her sudden thirst.

"'Twas a terrible dream," she whispered to herself.

But even as she told herself this, she wasn't comforted by the words. While she didn't remember the exact details of her dream, the feeling of dread lingered, digging its icy fingers into her flesh.

Darra pushed the damp hair from her face, and hooked the loose strands behind her ears. It was likely the storm that had awoken her. Harvest time was drawing to a close, yet the autumn storms continued to unleash its wrath on them.

A sudden gust of wind shook the shutters, causing her to shiver. When she had awoken, a thin sheen of sweat had formed on her forehead, but the crisp night air cooled it, leaving her feeling clammy and chilled. Even the velvet curtains surrounding her bed were ineffective in keeping out the cold air, or the terrors of the night. Each time her maid Fyfa closed the thick curtains, Darra usually felt safe and secure.

But not tonight.

Scanning the hanging fabric, she searched for any holes in the protective barrier. She frowned when she couldn't find any obvious breach. Shaking her head, she tried to cast aside the strange sense that something was not right. Whatever dark dream that haunted her had somehow passed into her consciousness, leaving her shaken and scared. The only small comfort she had was that her maid slept just on the other side of the curtains. She held her breath for half a second, listening to the maid's soft snores. But her relief was brief.

Somehow her mind continued to race at a warped speed, and she found it impossible to fall back asleep. Pulling the woolen blanket up and wrapping it around her shoulders, she knew full well that it wasn't warmth that she sought. For some reason her world felt insecure. Nay, she corrected herself, her world was insecure for a long while now. And she blamed the shaky foundation on her father's untimely death. Her mother, while she lived, drifted through the castle in a trance, as if she pined for the day when she would join her husband. The grief that covered Lady Venora Lochclay was like a great shroud, and no one could penetrate the barrier, not even Darra.

Before tragedy struck, her mother was the castle healer who was renowned and revered. She was willing and eager to assist anyone that sought her help, and people from near and far came to see her.

Her father was a brave and loyal knight who lost his life while fighting to serve his king. When Sir Arthur Berchelaine died in battle, his funeral was well attended by the local gentry and even a royal representative was present. He was given the fanfare that was due to a respected knight who died in honor of his king. But that honor did nothing to change the fact that he was dead. Her mother had shut down emotionally, and left Darra to fend for herself.

She clenched the blanket, remembering the loneliness, despair and anger at how her parents had abandoned her.

A week after her father's death, Fyfa found her in the solar. "The people are waiting for ye in the great hall, milady."

Darra turned away from the window. She had cried enough to fill the moat that surrounded Lancullin Castle.

"Why are they here?" she said tiredly.

The maid creased her brows and frowned slightly. "They've come for healing of course."

"Well, tell them that I cannot help them." She went back to staring out the window. "They will have to wait until my mother is well again, or they can go seek help from the town healer."

"The witch has taken ill, milady," Fyfa said, chewing at her bottom lip. "And besides, I'm only a servant; the people will nae listen tae me. Ye will have tae go tell them yourself." She wrung her hands together, as if she debated whether she should speak her piece. Then finally, she said, "Go tae them, milady. At the moment, ye are their hope."

Darra's eyes fastened onto the hills in the horizon, although she wasn't seeing anything. She didn't want to be anyone's hope. Not when her own life felt so wretched.

The hands in her lap curled into fists. She was aware of the tightness across her shoulder blades and the tiny fear that festered beneath her breast. "My mother is the healer," she said in a low voice. "I am only seventeen years old, an apprentice. My lady mother has not taught —"

"She has taught ye enough," Fyfa said, interrupting. "Ye have the blood of great healers running through your veins, milady." She gentled her voice. "As ye ken, your mother is felled by grief. She cannae heal others when she cannae heal herself. Now 'tis your duty tae care for the sick."

Darra was silent.

"Please, milady," Fyfa said, laying her hands on Darra's sleeve. "Your mother needs more time. Someone must lead us while she heals from her heartache."

But what about my heartache? she wanted to ask. *Do I not need more time to grieve as well?*

Fyfa pressed her palms tightly together in front of her chest, an imploring expression on her countenance. Two times a month, Lady Venora opened the castle gates to the sick, and they came in droves, seeking remedies for their many ailments. If Darra didn't go below stairs, the people would be rebuffed and some of them would die.

"You are right," she said, letting out a long sigh. "Someone must take charge. But once Mother is recovered, I will withdraw."

But that was a year ago, and Lady Venora was still not recovered. And since someone had to continue healing the sick, the responsibility fell on Darra's shoulders. After a time, she found the work satisfying, and took pride in helping the sick become whole again.

The only worrisome consideration was her mother. Lady Venora persevered to flit through the castle as if she was a ghost, however lately she had also become obsessed with death and dying. Her mother's insistence in speaking about the subjects truly frightened Darra. People were known to commit suicide while in they were in the throes of grief. Was her mother at this juncture? All at once, she felt an urgency to find a cure for her mother's despondency. She wasn't certain whether it was possible to treat the illness of spirit, but she owed it to her mother to try. After all, her mother was the only family member she had left.

With her mission firmly set in her mind, she spent the entire day pouring over the old manuals that were stored in the solar. She went through every herbal book, searching for that elusive antidote. And when she was about to give up on her search, a passage struck her.

Sol terrestris: A treasured plant for healing deep inner wounds.

She traced her finger over the golden petals of the drawing, its stamens radiating like the rays of the sun. Why not? The author didn't specify the type of inner wound in which it was used. But even though her mother's wounds weren't physical, they still ran deep. Perhaps this little plant was the healing elixir that she was searching for.

Closing the book with a thud, she tucked it under her arm and ran to find Fyfa. While she wasn't allowed to leave the castle grounds without an escort, she soon found a guard willing to take them to the meadow just outside the castle gates. With her book in hand, she bent at the waist, scouring the land in search for the flowers. And when she saw the plants sticking out of a mound of earth, its yellow petals opened to catch the sun's warmth, a giddiness came over her. She was certain that this plant would help lift her mother's spirit. And then finally, she would have her mother back.

When Darra collected enough of the delicate petals, she took them to the castle kitchen. Stealing a pot from the cook, she boiled the blooms in sweet wine. When the golden hue from the petals seeped into the liquid, coloring it into a rich, coppery amber, she strained it into a waiting bottle. Then with a light heart, she took her gift to her mother.

Except her mother didn't want her gift, and ignored Darra's outstretched hand. All the excitement she experienced earlier crashed to the floor, shattering at her feet.

"Why will you not try the medicine, mother?" she asked, fighting back the wave of disappointment, yet it still managed to creep into her voice.

"I do not need it," her mother said, her voice wane. "I am fine."

You are not fine! she wanted to scream, but she refrained herself. She placed the bottle on the side table. A healer's creed was not to force a remedy onto a person. That was the one thing that her mother drilled into her during her apprenticeship. And it was something that she had to respect. In her experience, she saw how ineffective a remedy was when a person was forced to take it.

A loud clap of thunder suddenly sounded in Darra's chamber, jerking her out of her thoughts, and reminding her of her present circumstance.

Letting out a long breath, she flattened her hand on the blanket and smoothed out the wrinkles. How odd it was for her to be contemplating her mother at this ungodly hour. Barely a few hours ago she saw Lady Venora at the Michaelmas feast in the great hall. Now the reveling and festivities were finished, everyone, including her mother, should be in bed, fast asleep. Clearly there was nothing wrong here. There was no reason for her to be dwelling on her mother.

Still, the strange and persistent urging was hard to ignore, and she crawled over to the edge of the mattress. It was doubtful that she could return to sleep unless she satisfied her curiosity and determined that everything was all right.

When she parted the curtain that surrounded the four-poster bed, the chilly air blasted her and almost sent her back into her protective cocoon.

The fire in the hearth was long dead, but she could make out the dark outline of her maid sleeping on the pallet next to her bed. Her gaze slid past the maid, searching for an alternative explanation as to why her sleep was disturbed. But there was nothing.

Dropping her foot down over the edge of the bed, she felt for the slipper that was usually placed there. The cold air skimmed her exposed calf, forcing a hiss to escape from her lips. She could almost convince herself that she was worrying needlessly, and that she would be better off crawling back under the covers. Except the voice inside her head continued to push her forward. When her foot slipped into the other slipper, Fyfa stirred and flipped onto her side, facing Darra. As if she somehow sensed that something was amiss, she opened her eyes and abruptly sat up.

"Milady?" she asked, her voice still groggy with sleep. "What are ye doing out of your bed?"

"'Tis nothing Fyfa," she said. "Go back to sleep."

Fyfa stretched her arms in the air and let out a big yawn. "'Tis too late, I'm already awake." Her tone became suspicious. "Are ye going somewhere, milady?" she asked.

Darra sighed. A number of possible answers entered her head, but Fyfa wouldn't believe any of them; the maid knew her too well to be fooled. Fyfa had become a constant, loyal companion from the moment she entered into the family's service. She was four years older than Darra, and helped to alleviate the seclusion of living without the friendship of girls her age. But of course because of her familiarity, she spoke candidly and without censure. Such as now.

"Well?" Fyfa asked.

"If you must know, I am going to see my mother."

"At this time of night?" Doubt crept into her voice. "Lady Venora would be asleep — just as ye should be, milady. Besides, your mother would have barred her bed chamber door." She plopped her head back on her pillow as if the discussion was over, and she fully expected Darra to go back to bed.

"Sometimes Lady Venora leaves her door unlocked," she said, tugging the woolen blanket off her bed and draping it over her shoulders. "I will check on her. If her door is locked then I will be back soon enough."

Fyfa groaned, pushed herself to a standing position, and dragged her blanket across her thin shoulders as well. "Milady, ye ken I cannae allow ye tae go by yourself." She let out another loud yawn. Staggering over to the side table, she fumbled to light the candle there. Then gripping the pewter candle holder, she moved past Darra. "I will go first tae light the way."

The silence was almost deafening as they entered the dark corridor, while her thoughts became loud and unrelenting. Why was she wandering around in the middle of the night? If her mother was awake, she would likely be displeased to discover Darra in her chamber. But Darra had already gone so far, and it seemed foolish to turn back.

When they finally arrived at the oak door, Fyfa lifted the candle holder so Darra could find the handle. She was about to push at the door open when she paused at hearing the murmuring voices from inside. She gave Fyfa an alarmed glance.

"What is it, milady?" Fyfa whispered as she bent closer, her wide eyes illuminated by the candlelight.

Darra waved a hand to silence the maid. Putting her palm on the rough panel, she leaned in to place an ear at the door. She took a sharp intake of breath and abruptly jerked back.

"Get the guards," she hissed. "There is a man in Lady Venora's bed chamber!"

Chapter 2

❧

"But what will ye do, milady?" Fyfa asked, gripping the candle holder tightly. The glow of the candle lit her face, magnifying her fear.

"I need to know why there is a man in my mother's bed chamber," Darra said tightly. "I told you to fetch the guards."

"I dinnae think 'tis a guid idea tae go in there," she said, once again ignoring Darra's command. Her maid shifted uncomfortably on her bare feet, sending a look of longing at the direction of Darra's bed chamber. She gathered the edges of her blanket to her neck. "Perhaps 'tis a trick of the mind, and ye are tired, milady. After all, ye attended mass early this morn, and then ye had tae partake in the Michaelmas festivities…"

Darra shook her head, not wanting to waste time in idle conversation while her mother was in possible danger. Whether or not it was wise to enter the chamber, she didn't care. It was out of character for Lady Venora to entertain men in her room. Perhaps other widows did this, but not her mother. Without waiting to see if Fyfa left to do her bidding, she pushed at the door handle. She let out a hiss of relief when there was no resistance. Her mother had forgotten to bar her door again.

Her palms felt clammy and cold although it wasn't the cool night air that affected her. For a moment she stood still, clutching at the blanket that was wrapped around her shoulders. The sound of the blood rushing through her veins and the thunderous roar of her pounding heart filled her ears. The noise was so loud that she feared that the intruder inside would hear it. But even as she took a step forward and slipped through the door, no one accosted her.

Relief flooded her, and she surveyed the bed chamber, which was dimly lit by the candle on the dressing table near her mother's bed.

But then Darra saw *him,* and she staggered back against the wall, her entire body pressed flushed against it. Of all people to find in her mother's chamber, he wasn't what she had imagined at all. He wasn't dressed like an ordinary Englishman. In fact, he wasn't English at all but a devil Scot. And he was large, larger than any man that she had ever encountered. At the moment he was turned the other way. She could see his flame colored hair and his broad, muscular back, where a menacing claymore was strapped. Part of his great kilt draped loosely along his masculine back, while the lower portion of the plaid hugged his narrow hips, dropping to the back of his knees, and exposing strong and powerful calves. Even from this vantage point, she could sense the air of lethal danger that crackled around him, an air that clearly marked him as a warrior. What sort of defense did she have against a brawny man of this magnitude? The deadly brute could snap her and her mother as easily as if they were twigs. She swallowed hard, and prayed that Fyfa would hurry back with the castle guards.

His attention was trained onto her mother even as he moved into the warm candlelight. Shifting his body slightly to the side, his visage came into view. For a split second her breath caught in her throat as she stared at his rugged male beauty. But before any noise escaped, she clapped a hand over her mouth.

She shook her head. This was not an opportune time to gawk at the comely interloper. His lips continued to move, and he waved a hand in a languid gesture as if he was conducting a normal, everyday conversation in the great hall. Except he was in her mother's bed chamber — in the dead of the night.

Darra inched along the wall, her fingers skimming against the rough stone as she attempted to get close enough to overhear them. She needed to know his identity, and what he wanted from her mother.

The drapes around the bed were parted, but it was too dark to discern how her mother fared. Her poor, gentle mother was likely paralyzed with terror.

As she got closer, his Scottish lilt reached her ears, the sound almost like a gentle song. But then the meaning of his words penetrated her consciousness, and her heart lurched in alarm.

"I'm nae giving ye a choice, milady," he was saying to her mother. "Ye can come quietly or nae."

"I would rather kill myself than go with you," Lady Venora hissed.

Fear rose immediately to Darra's throat, threatening to choke her. Though her mother spoke quietly, there was deadly conviction in her tone. Her mother was in a fragile state. Would this intruder disrupt the fine thread that held her sanity intact?

She balled her hands into fists, wishing that she could clobber the large Highlander. How dare he come here and disturb her peace? Her father was already dead. She was not willing to see her mother die as well.

Searching frantically around for a weapon, her panicked mind also raced to formulate a plan to rescue her mother. Her eyes alighted on the ornamental broadswords that hung above the mantel a few paces from where she stood. The old swords hung on the wall with the blade edges crossing over one another. Right beneath the two swords, the shield with the family crest was proudly displayed.

The weapons had belonged to her father, but upon his death, Lady Venora insisted on showcasing them in her bed chamber. For many hours she sat at the chair near the hearth, staring at the swords as if they somehow provided a link to her dead husband. It was during these moments, that Darra despised the old swords, and she yearned to tear them down and throw them into the fire. But now, she realized, the ugly, hateful weapons would become useful.

All instincts urged her to dash across to the hearth and pull a sword off the wall. But she forced herself to bide her time and move at a slower, more careful pace. Even she could see that the sword was too distant, and the bold Highlander would seize her before she pulled the weapon free.

She flattened herself against the cold stone wall, intently watching the strapping Highlander as she sidled along, getting closer and closer to her target.

Darra was almost at the fireplace when her mother sat up suddenly and stared straight at her, a shocked expression etched upon her countenance. Darra gave a frantic shake to her head, silently entreating her not to betray her.

But it was already too late. The perceptive intruder noticed Lady Venora's momentary shock and pivoted to follow her line of sight. And then he saw Darra.

Get the sword! her mind screamed. Her internal instincts catapulted her into motion. The blanket on her shoulders dropped to the ground as she tore across the chamber to the hearth. Scrambling up on the chair, she grunted as she wrenched the sword from the wall. The resonance of metal sliding against stone reverberated across the room.

Exhilaration consumed her as she held the dangerous weapon in her hand. But that excitement soon waned when she staggered underneath its weight. She had seen the castle guards easily wield their swords, but she was ignorant over how heavy the weapons were in reality.

She jumped off the chair, the impact jarring her teeth. But she was determined not to show her terror, so she brought both hands to the grip. With her legs spread far apart and the heavy broadsword held in front of her, she found her balance.

"Move away from the bed," she said, pointing the sword tip at the large intruder.

"Who are ye?" Rory asked, studying the fierce angel that suddenly appeared out of no where.

The soft candlelight reflected off her golden tresses, while the flickering light cast shadows on her linen chemise, outlining her sweet, lush curves. A sudden desire seized him, and he wanted to pull off the shift and view her glorious nakedness.

"I know who I am." An angry flush rose to her cheeks. "But I do not know who you are." The broadsword in her hands lent her confidence, and she dared to walk closer to him.

Her oval visage was bathed in the soft light, showcasing her guileless beauty. Fair brows arched over stormy blue orbs, while her plump, sweet lips enticed him. If they had met in the bonny hills of Scotland, he would have readily taken her to his bed. Except they were in England, he reminded himself. A steely determination reflected in her dark blue eyes. And it was apparent that she would rather slice his torso than spend time in his arms.

But even so, his body reacted to her scent of sweet roses and sandalwood. It took all his willpower to refrain from reaching over to caress her soft cheek, and discovering whether or not she was a figment of his imagination.

"I said that you need to move away from the bed."

"Or what will ye do, lass?" he asked, barely suppressing a smile. Aside from his siblings, no one hazarded to challenge him in a long while. It amused him that this wee lass was courageous enough to stand up to him, even though he was a head taller and much stronger.

While there was an air of innocence that surrounded her, he sensed that a fire burned beneath the exterior. He took a small step forward, holding out his hand. "Why dinnae ye give me that broadsword before ye hurt yourself."

"Stay where you are!" she snarled. She gripped the sword tightly, swaying a bit before finding her footing again.

"See?" he said, trying his best to keep the amusement out of his voice, "That sword is much too big and cumbersome for a lass like yourself. Ye can barely hold onto the grip."

She obviously knew that he spoke the truth, but she raised her chin in defiance. Shifting her arms slightly to the side, she raised the sword and swung it over her shoulder. "Tell me who you are, and what you are doing in my mother's bed chamber," she said, her tone authoritative and cold.

"I'm Rory MacGregon, Chief of Clan MacGregon." He held out both of his palms, facing them outward just as he took a step closer. Since she had no plans to relinquish the weapon, he needed to distract her before either of them got hurt. "And I —"

"And I told *you* to stay where you are!" Her blue eyes flashed. "The guards have been alerted of your presence, and they will be here soon."

"Was this the lass who was supposed tae alert the guards?" a familiar voice asked at the doorway. "It looks like she cannae find them as she's all tied up at the moment." His brother Duncan pushed the maid further into the chamber, causing her to fall to her knees.

"Fyfa!" Darra cried. Concern and fear twisted in her countenance, and in her distraught state, she lowered her guard. It was only a small opening, but that was all he needed. Seizing the opportunity, he lunged at her.

"Lady Darra, watch out!" Fyfa said.

The lass was startled by the cry, but didn't react fast enough to her maid's warning. Rory knocked the sword from her grip, allowing the weapon to clatter harmlessly to the floor.

Darra blinked at it for a split second as if in shock before bending down to reach for it.

But he was already one step ahead of her. With his booted foot, he kicked the sword away to the far end of the chamber, the metal scraping across the stone surface. Then as she started to run across the room to retrieve the weapon, he hauled her close, pulling her tightly against his chest. She fought against him, squirming, straining, scratching in an attempt to free herself.

But she was much smaller than him, and he forced her back until she was braced against the wall, trapped between it and his body. With one hand he grabbed a hold of her wrists and pinned them above her head.

As his heavier frame shoved against her, her struggles slowed. But even though she was imprisoned, her breath heavy with exertion and her teeth bared, a rebellious fire burned from within her. He had never seen anything so breathtaking. And it was at that moment when she glanced up and latched onto his gaze. Something strange and alluring passed between them, and his movements ceased. An explosive awareness flared in her guileless blue orbs, an awareness that no doubt reflected in his own depths.

Her soft feminine body molded perfectly against his hardness, and he felt an intense surge of desire rushing to his groin. He wanted to dip his head and bury it into the hollow of her neck, breathing in her pure, intoxicating scent.

He hooded his eyes and nudged her legs apart, settling himself at her center. Taking in a deep breath, he savored the sweet sensation of being cradled between her rounded hips. There was not much material between them and his cock swelled at that knowledge.

A rosy flush that started at the neckline of her chemise began to spread like wildfire across her smooth, velvety skin. With every breath she took, her chest heaved, but slowly her breathing changed into pants. She was a mixture of fear, confusion and curiosity.

His gaze swept down and settled on her lush, moist lips, and he wondered how she would taste. It had been far too long since he last bedded a lass, and that part of him stirred, fully acknowledging his observation.

Rory was so mesmerized by the soft woman crushed against him that he didn't notice that someone sneaked behind him. And that was when he felt a sudden intense pain radiating across his back. He arched his spine and gasped. Whipping his head around, he angled to see who attacked him.

"Get off my daughter, you bastard!" Venora hissed.

The captivating lass trapped against him leaned her head to the side, studying her mother. Her shocked expression suggested that even she didn't recognize the witch wielding the iron poker.

Venora lifted the poker over her head, ready to strike again, but Duncan fortunately intervened, and pulled the offending item from her grip.

The lady of the castle let out a cry of outrage, and directed her attack on Duncan. Unfortunately for her, the only weapons she possessed were her small fists, and they easily glanced off Rory's brother.

"Bastards," she hissed.

Duncan caught the woman and restrained her hands behind her back.

"I thought ye said this would be a simple task," he said.

"So I was wrong," Rory let out a groan. "Tie her up before she permanently maims me."

He turned his attention back to the delectable lass who was still pinned against him.

"If only ye were nae an English lass," he murmured regretfully. Taking a piece of rope from his sporran, he quickly bounded her wrists. As soon as he was finished, he pulled away from her.

"Put her with the others," he grunted to Duncan.

Placing a forearm against the wall, he leaned his head on it, waiting for the stabbing pain to subside. He groaned a little when he twisted around to watch Duncan guide the lass over to where her mother and maid huddled together.

Darra stared at Rory, her expressive eyes filled with contempt. In fact, she regarded him as if he ate wee bairns for dinner. But what did he care about what an English lass thought of him? He shook off the unsettling question. This vixen who appeared out of nowhere was single-handedly complicating things. Dawn was a few hours away, yet they were still here.

He turned to his brother. "Have ye checked if there are any others lurking about?"

"Aye," Duncan said, "I searched before I returned tae this bed chamber and found nay one else."

Darra watched distractedly as the formidable men moved away from them. They spoke in low tones and she could barely make out what they said. Truthfully though, she wasn't concentrating on their conversation. Her mind was in the past, playing over and over again the moment that she was compressed against Rory's hard planes. She had tried her best to fight him off, but her attempts were futile. The Highlander was easily over six feet tall, and he was much more powerful than she.

There was also that curious energy that passed between them. It made her knees unsteady. If he hadn't supported her with his weight, she would have likely collapsed into a mushy heap on the ground.

She couldn't understand what came over her. The feelings were foreign, scary and thrilling all at once. When he glanced down at her, a part of her wondered how it would feel to have his firm, masculine lips pressed to hers. And as she thought that, time seemed to stop, and she even forgot the reason why she entered her mother's bed chamber in the first place. It was fortunate that her mother struck the Highlander when she did, for that attack broke the spell that held her captive.

Aye, it was a spell that he casted over her and nothing more. She was a level-headed woman, and didn't have time to entertain wanton thoughts. Darra directed her attention back to the men. But her thoughts froze suddenly when the words *Scotland* and *dangerous* reached her ears.

She glanced over at her mother, a streak of fear running down her spine. The Highlanders were intent on taking her away from here.

But the crazed bravado Lady Venora demonstrated moments ago had transformed her. She wasn't watching Darra but stared intently at the Highlanders. Who was this woman? She certainly wasn't the gentle mother that Darra knew. Her hair was in disarray, and there was a wild, caged look in her eyes. Was the shock at witnessing barbarians in her chamber too much for her to handle, and was she now losing her faculties? If the intruders dragged Lady Venora away from Lancullin Castle, then Darra worried that her mother would find a way to end her own life...

"You cannot take my mother to Scotland," Darra said loudly, causing both men to assess her. She stared at the rugged chief, knowing full well that she was at a disadvantage. After all she was the one that was tied up and on the ground. Still, it was her duty to protect her mother and keep her safe.

"Be nae concerned," Rory said, a sympathetic look reflected briefly in his green depths. Then as if suddenly remembering that she was his enemy, his expression changed and his brows slanted down with irritation. "Lady Venora will come back tae ye once her purpose is finished."

"What purpose?" Darra glanced from Rory to her mother. She was missing something here. For some reason he seemed to know Lady Venora, however from her recollection, she had never heard of the MacGregons. But then again, her mother neglected to speak much about her Scottish heritage.

"He means to take me to heal the dying Eanruing MacGregon, Darra," she said, her voice tight with anger. "But I would kill myself rather than heal that — that devil."

Darra's eyes widened as she watched her mother. Hearing the unwavering conviction behind her mother's words confirmed her worst suspicions. And that fear took a hold of her, curling in her belly, expanding and contracting in time to the erratic thudding of her heart.

Rory frowned at Lady Venora as if he heard the finality in her voice as well. "Nay, ye willnae kill yourself, milady. We've come all this way tae get ye, sae we'll nae be going back empty-handed."

"You would force my mother to go with you even when 'tis clear that she is in a fragile state?" Darra asked incredulously.

Rory's gaze shifted to her. "Aye, if need be."

Her heart plummeted at hearing his ruthless honesty. The firm, sculpted line of his jaw became rigid and stubborn, and any warmth he expressed earlier was gone. No words came to mind, and all she could do was gape at him in disbelief. She had heard of these cold, unfeeling savages from the north. Little did she know that all the stories, all the rumors that she learned were true. And the man that exemplified these undesirable qualities stood before her.

"You heard my mother." Darra pushed herself up from the floor and faced him, her hands still restrained. "If you take her by force, then 'tis assured that she will end her life." *And all will be lost to me.* She took in one shuddering breath before she straightened to her full height and tilted her chin in the air. "I cannot have this. You must take me instead."

Chapter 3

కింഷ

"And why should I take ye?" Rory asked, folding his powerful arms across his chest.

"I am a healer too," Darra said in a rush. "My mother has taught me everything she knows. In fact people from all over come to me when they are sick."

"Milady!" Fyfa hissed.

But both Rory and Darra ignored the maid. He regarded Lady Venora before shifting his focus on to Darra, his expression becoming thoughtful. "And ye have experience with fevers?"

"Aye." Relief flooded her as she realized that he was contemplating her offer. All she needed was to lure them out of the stronghold, and then escape them once they let down their guard. She stretched her lips into a thin smile. "I cure fevers all the time."

Rory gave a curt nod and untied her wrists. "I'll accompany ye tae your bed chamber sae ye can gather your things."

"Wait," Fyfa said quickly. "Milady will need me tae help her pack."

He shot the maid an annoyed glance, and appeared as if he was about to refuse her, but then he said, "Fine." He turned to his brother. "Duncan, ye stay here with Lady Venora."

Darra could feel the blood drain from her face. "Will you give me your word that your kin will not harm my mother?"

His eyes glittered coldly. "Nae if ye cross me."

Darra nodded slowly, although it wasn't one of acquiesce. She needed to be cautious with this man.

Fyfa went to fetch the candle holder and led the way to Darra's bed chamber.

"'Tis nae a guid idea for ye tae go with them, milady," Fyfa said under her breath. A small draft in the dark corridor caused the candlelight to waver slightly. "The MacGregons are dangerous."

"How do you know of them?"

Fyfa threw a furtive glance over her shoulder. Satisfied that Rory was far enough away, she continued, "If ye are from the highlands, ye ken. They're one of the most dominant clans to the east, and their brute strength and wild ways are known throughout the land." She paused as if to emphasize her last point. "Nae many men can cross a MacGregon, and live tae brag about it."

Darra moved past her maid and pushed open her bed chamber door.

Her mind whirled as Fyfa's dire warning sunk in. Her decision to lure these strangers away from the castle no longer seemed like a viable idea. But you had no choice, a voice inside her insisted. And she really had no choice. It was her duty to watch over her mother. If her father was still alive, he would have done the same. Yet there was also a small, selfish part of her that didn't want to be left alone in this world. Her mother was all she had.

She scanned her bed chamber, not wanting to take along any of her possessions, since she had no intentions of going to Scotland. But the Highlander was watching her, and she had to demonstrate eager compliance.

She bent down to pick up her medicine basket that was beside the table.

"I will need my gown," she said to Fyfa.

Her maid ran obediently to fetch the woolen gown from the ornate trunk which sat at the foot of Darra's bed.

Glancing wistfully at the door where the Highlander stood guard, she wished that she had the nerve to scream. At least then the guards would be alarmed and would run to save her. But of course chaos would ensue and everyone in the vicinity would be endangered. After last night's drinking and feasting, the garrison was bound to be sloppy, and the much larger and sober Highlanders would easily defeat them.

"Do not fret, Fyfa," she said in a low voice, and smiled at her with a bravery that she didn't feel. "When the guards are alerted of my disappearance, they will find me."

She twisted her hands in her apron. "I'll notify the guards as soon as I can, milady."

"What are the two of ye blathering about?" Rory glowered at them. "If ye have gathered all your things then we'll leave now."

His tone caused a rush of anger to swirl in her gut. She thrust back her shoulders, and sent him a haughty look. "You are dragging me away from my home, and in the middle of the night," she reminded him. "Because of the chill in the air, I cannot go in my chemise."

"Hurry up then," he snapped and presented his broad back to give her privacy.

"How will the castle guards find ye, milady?" Fyfa whispered.

She lifted her arms in the air, and with quick efficiency, the maid slipped the gown on her and laced the material.

"Perhaps I can run away from my captors, and the guards will not need to rescue me," Darra answered, her lips barely moving. She then reached over, and gave her maid's hand a reassuring squeeze. "I vow that I will be free of them in one way or another."

"Are ye done yet?" he said, impatience evident in his voice.

Darra swallowed as she glanced over at the brawny man who stood at the threshold. She recalled how easily he towered over her. And her traitorous body recollected only too well how his hard length pressed against her.

"Aye," she said.

He let out an exaggerated sigh of relief. "'Tis about time," he muttered, and herded them back to Lady Venora's bed chamber.

"I'll take the lass while ye stay here with the lady, and the maid," Rory said as soon as they walked into the room. He jerked his chin at Darra. "I dinnae want this one tae get any ideas about fleeing."

***

A thick silence followed them as Rory gripped her elbow, and led Darra through the dark corridor and then down the serpentine steps.

She slanted her eyes at the man who walked beside her, but the only thing that she could discern was the shadowy outline of his profile. For a lethal man, he moved quietly, as if he was used to maneuvering in the darkness. Was she unwittingly leading herself to her own demise? She shuddered at that last thought. This could very well be the last time she walked the corridors of Lancullin Castle.

Rory's familiarity with the castle layout suggested that he had been here before, scoping out the lay of the castle. But why didn't Sir Jarin, the garrison commander, ferret out the intruder? It disturbed her to think that the castle defenses were so easily breached.

Reaching out, she touched the rough, cold wall, steadying herself as she descended the last of the winding steps.

She wished that there was something, *someone* that would stop them on the way to the great hall.

Unfortunately her wish was as empty as the great hall itself. The servants were retired to their quarters, and the castle guards were slumbering in their barracks. Meanwhile her mother and maid were upstairs, tied up and their fates unknown. The uncertainty and fear for her loved ones caused a tight, almost painful band to form across her shoulders. She didn't know anything about these men, and Fyfa's warning rang grimly in her head.

All too soon, they cleared the great hall, and she heard Rory breathe a sigh of relief. He beckoned for her to come forward, and she forced her feet to move even though her instincts urged her to spin around and take flight. Except she knew that running off would make her dilemma worse. He would simply return to Lady Venora's bed chamber, and drag her away instead. That risk caused gooseflesh to prickle along her arms, and she lifted her hands to rub them away.

A few more steps, and they entered the deserted courtyard. She dragged her icy fingers across her forehead, pushing away the wayward strands of hair.

The storm was finished, and the air smelled of damp earth and rain. During the day, the courtyard was filled with activity and noise, with servants engaged in their chores, and the animals let loose to roam. Now nothing but a thunderous silence remained.

Taking a hold of her arm, he bent his head and murmured in her ear, "This way tae the stable, lass."

She felt his fevered breath on her skin, and a strange warmth coursed through her system. Irritation gripped her while her body continued to hum in reaction to his nearness.

"I know where the stable is," she said sharply.

Darra yanked her arm away from his touch. Her violent motion caused him to release her in surprise. Stumbling back, her foot crushed down on something behind her. A loud shriek filled the night air.

She jumped and gasped at the startling noise. Then before she could fully recover from her fright, a cat that was partially hidden behind a barrel, rounded on her, swiping at her tender skin with its sharp claws, and drawing blood. A stabbing pain shot to her ankle. And when she reached to press at the throbbing area, a mouse burst out of its hiding place from among the barrels. The movement was unexpected, and triggered an innate panic within her. As the vermin throttled toward her, a scream started to form in her throat.

But Rory, having anticipated her reaction, quickly clamped a hand over her mouth, smothering her cry. He pulled her tightly against his hard chest, his embrace protective and secure. Meanwhile the hairs on the cat bristled as its spine arched. Drawing back its lips, it let out a loud, threatening hiss before it wheeled, and bounded after its quarry.

The pain in her ankle faded as the warmth from Rory's solid build seeped in and obliterated her fear. For the length of a heart beat, she allowed herself to melt into his heat. She was tempted, oh so tempted to stay in his protective embrace, to once again meld her softness into his unyielding length. But Rory was her enemy, not her savior. Through sheer willpower, she placed both palms on his chest and pushed away.

She felt the blood rush to her face, and was glad for the shadows that hid her burning cheeks.

"Are ye hurt?" he said into her ear. The soft burr of his voice sent a shiver down to her belly, causing a peculiar stir. A sudden warmth blanketed her. And her brain froze momentarily as she caught the faint smell of soap, and something else that she couldn't place.

Darra nodded, unable to do anything else and he dropped his hand from her mouth. He surprised her further by bending down and sliding up her gown to expose her ankle.

"'Tis hardly a scratch," he murmured. The contrasting sensation of cool air hitting her flushed skin, and his warm touch made her feel light-headed. He stood up. "Ye will not perish."

Sucking in an unsteady breath, she somehow managed to keep her heart from bursting out of her chest. She was doing a noble deed, she reminded herself. She was taking the kidnappers away from her mother. That notion managed to calm her racing heart. Catastrophe would be averted, and her mother, indeed the entire occupants of the castle, would be safe. That was all that mattered.

Rory placed his hand at the small of her back and guided her toward the stable. And this time, she didn't protest.

They were almost at the entrance when he suddenly veered to the right, leading her to a cart that was loaded with hay.

He surveyed the area as if he was searching for someone or something. From where she stood, she could see the dark outline of the stable, and nothing else.

"Psst! Over here, Rory!" a voice hissed.

She caught Rory's relieved expression. A second later, he dragged her closer to the cart, to where a burly man awaited.

As she neared the transport, her nose twitched. She was about to make a comment when Rory cursed aloud.

"Why do I smell shit, Griogair?"

The dark-haired man shrugged his muscled shoulders. "Sorry, this was the best I could do, Rory. The man was cleaning out the stables when I came upon him. I knocked him out, and tied him up." He peered curiously at her and frowned as he scanned her from head to foot. He turned to Rory and quirked a questioning brow. "What's this? I thought the healer was an auld woman, nae a bonny lass like this one."

"There was a change in plans," Rory said shortly. "Get us out of here before the sky starts tae lighten. If we leave at present, we'll have at least nine hours head start."

"But where's Duncan?" The large Highlander folded his massive arms and frowned at his companion.

"He's staying behind tae ensure that nay trouble arises." Rory's cool gaze fell on to her, and she shivered.

"A head start is a guid idea," Griogair agreed. "Duncan will track us down later. Once we get tae the Scottish borders, the castle garrison will nae be able tae keep up with us in the craggy terrain."

"There is truth in that," he said. "Come, lass," he beckoned to her. "I'll help ye up onto the cart."

She recoiled and took a step back as if he told her to leap out of a window. "You do not mean for me to get onto that cart, do you?" she asked, unable to keep the horror out of her voice. A man from the town came once a month to transport the dirty hay out of the castle. She had never given it much thought as to where it was taken, or when. All she knew was that the stable was cleaned, and the old hay was replaced by new sweet smelling straw.

"Aye, that is exactly what I mean. Ye better —" He cut himself off and jerked his head at his brother.

Before she could determine what was happening, Griogair dove underneath the cart. At the same time, Rory flattened his palm over her mouth, effectively preventing any noise from escaping. Then with his other hand, he wrapped it around her waist, and hauled her up onto the cart. While holding her firmly against his hard body, he tugged at the excess material of his plaid, and wrapped it around them both before diving into the dirty hay. He had just enough time to bury them deeper into the straw when she heard someone coughing in the distance.

Rory's hand was still over her mouth, and his emerald eyes glittered dangerously.

"Dinnae move, or make a sound," Rory said, his voice barely above a whisper.

Darra wasn't sure if there was a threat laced in his words, but she didn't mean to find out. She nodded, even as her heart pounded heavily in her chest. There was too much at risk if she crossed the fierce Highlander.

She sensed him staring at her for a long moment, and then slowly he released his grip over her mouth.

Another cough rang out, and she surmised that whoever was out there was not far from where they hid. There was tension in Rory's large frame, and it tensed even more when the man outside the cart let out a curse. That obscenity had a different effect on Darra.

It was Sir Jarin; she was certain of it. But what was the garrison commander doing out at this time of night?

An instant later, the answer to that question became apparent when a woman joined him.

"*You're late,*" Sir Jarin said.

"*I'm sorry, sire,*" the woman said, breathlessly. "*Some people in the servants' barracks were still awake, and I couldn't get away.*"

He let out a grunt and then a long moment of silence ensued. Just when Darra thought that the couple had left, she heard a soft purring. During the day, the noise might have been dismissed, but at night, the sound echoed in the still, crisp air, adding an unexpected heat.

Then suddenly the commotion was closer, as if the couple were embracing right next to them. A chill ran through her limbs. She could hear their heavy panting. And the moaning which was punctuated with a giggle became frenetic gasps. All the while the sounds grew more harsh and amplified.

She could feel the tips of her ears burn as she made the mortifying deduction of exactly what was happening nearby.

When Rory had grabbed her earlier, he had thrown himself first into the hay so that her descent would be cushioned. But now as she lay on top of his taut build, she was aware of every male inch of him, aware that her breasts were pressed tightly against his broad, muscular chest. And even though he wore a short jacket, she could feel the toned, hard brawn beneath her palm, an indisputable indication that he was no stranger to combat.

She could hear and feel his hot breath just above her. One corded arm was wrapped around her waist while the other one held the plaid over their heads. Though he didn't move, the place that he touched scorched through her clothing.

It shamed her to know how her body betrayed her. As the erotic din vibrated in her ears, her skin pricked with awareness. She was mindful of Rory's hard ridges underneath her. And unable to control it, her nipples hardened, while an inexplicable languid sensation swirled within her.

The air beneath Rory's excess plaid became unbearably hot. Even though she wanted to move, to get far, far away from this handsome Highlander, she kept her head on his chest. And as the fevered passions raged on the other side of the wooden panels, she could hear and feel the rapid thudding of Rory's heart. Then all at once she felt something growing, jabbing at her thighs.

Her heart began its own frantic race. The continued soft panting and cries of ecstasy from the lovers affected her more than she realized. She had treated many people, and knew the workings of a man's bodily parts. Most of all, she recognized what that insistent bulge against her legs meant. She should have been embarrassed by hearing the intimate mating sounds of the man and woman. But a curiosity took a hold of her, a curiosity that never showed itself until now. What did it feel like to kiss as passionately as these lovers? Darra had only experienced wet, sloppy pecks from would-be suitors. She was certain that kissing Rory would be different. But what exactly happened after an ardent, feverish kiss? Was the mating between a man and a woman similar to that of animals? Or was there something more?

The side of the cart creaked and began to rock. Then suddenly the amorous movements stopped.

"I cannot continue," Sir Jarin complained. *"All I can smell is horse shit."*

"Maybe we can go to the walled garden, and finish up?" the woman's thin, reedy voice purred.

The cart squeaked and moved as if a weight lifted from it.

"Aye, let's go."

More movements and then a long silence.

"Rory!" a voice hissed. "They're gone."

Slowly Rory released the hand that was around her waist. As he sat up, he brought her to a seated position as well. The heated spell that they shared seemed to evaporate into the night air, and she felt a strange sense of loss.

Griogair crawled out from underneath the cart. "That was close," he said.

"Aye, too close." Rory said. "Get this contraption rolling, and get us the hell out of here."

Chapter 4

⤞⤝

As they rounded a bend, Griogair let out a yell, urging the pack horse to move faster. The cart lurched forward, and Darra reached to grasp the wooden rail to keep herself from toppling over. It was almost too easy how they crossed through the castle gates. The guards barely paid attention to the cart or its contents, allowing Griogair to pass through with ease. Anger and frustration simmered within her. When she returned, she would definitely need to speak to Sir Jarin about this lax in the castle defenses.

The transport continued to hurtle along, her slight frame jostled by every bump on the uneven dirt road. This was not the situation that she thought she would find herself in when she went to sleep last night. If only she hadn't allowed her inquisitiveness to sway her. But of course she knew that her inner voice was difficult to ignore. It had served her too well in the past. And if she dismissed it, her mother would be in her place right now, facing untold dangers.

She didn't know how long they traveled, but eventually, the cart slowed down to a more reasonable pace.

Darra sat up and plucked out the straw that stuck to her hair. Glad to be free of the stifling heat from the hay, she took in a deep, fortifying breath of brisk air. She scanned the trees, taking in the dense forest. She imagined that there would at least be one opening for escape, but they had ridden for about an hour, and still no opportunity had presented itself. If they crossed to the Scottish borders, she perceived that she would have difficulty returning home. Not only would the distance be a problem, but she also had to avoid the highwaymen and outlaws who usually waylaid unsuspecting victims. That consideration left her feeling uneasy, and she groped for something to keep her mind off the peril that awaited her. Perhaps conversing with Rory would keep her distracted, and she might glean information that would aid her escape.

"How long will it take to arrive in Sco — at your home?" She couldn't bring herself to name his homeland because it sounded so final, as if she might actually go there.

"Three days," Rory said, rolling his shoulders, and then bending his neck from side to side to stretch it. However despite his casual demeanor, he was alert. His eyes continually scoured the passing forest as if he expected something ferocious to come out and attack them. Before she had a chance to inquire about what he was searching for, the cart suddenly careened to the left, the unexpected movement throwing her off balance. His strong, muscular arms caught her. While he stopped her fall, his sinewy forearm grazed the side of her breast. A current of energy passed through her, an energy that was intense and steady and which left her feeling simultaneously hot and cold. He peered down at her, his surprised expression suggesting that he felt the electric tension as well.

Time seemed to stand still as their eyes clashed, and she lost her ability to breathe. The area that he touched tingled and burned.

Griogair let out a sudden shout, ending the sorcery that circled her and Rory.

"I am sorry," she mumbled over the roar of rushing blood echoing in her ears. Why was she so attracted to Rory? True enough, he was a captivating man with a fine physique. But it didn't make any sense to her. Rory was her captor, her country's enemy. Apparently none of that mattered when he was near. He scarcely had to touch her, and a liquid heat swirled up and down her length.

"Are ye all right?"

She nodded. The last thing she wanted was for him to think that she deliberately threw herself at him. Taking a shaky breath, she pulled away from him just as the cart came to a complete stop.

"Get the horses, Griogair." Rory gestured to a moss covered boulder.

"Aye," Griogair jumped down from his seat. He walked a short distance, and disappeared behind the large rock.

A few minutes later, he emerged with two horses in tow. Now in the morning light, she had a clear view of the other man. While his brother was fair, Griogair was dark and solidly built; his muscles strained underneath his jacket while his powerful calves peeked out from beneath his plaid. The family resemblance was obvious, and both men were comely in their different ways.

She studied their clothing, and noted that these Highlanders didn't appear to come from wealth. While their great kilts and other clothing were well made, the materials were old and worn. They had a number of items attached to their belts, from a dirk to a small leather pouch that hung loosely at the center of their kilts. In addition to that, they possessed dangerous swords that they strapped to their backs. Suddenly she was reminded that she was among lethal warriors, and she needed to tread carefully.

"Will I be riding the pack horse?" she asked, her tone cautious.

"Nay, ye will be riding with me," Rory said. "The pack horse will stay here with the cart. The auld horse is too exhausted, and willnae survive traversing the Scottish terrain." He jumped off the cart. "Come," he said, offering her his hand.

"I can dismount by myself," she said, shaking her head. She didn't want him touching her again. Not when every contact with him threw her off kilter.

But she moved too slowly for him. Before she could protest, he wrapped his large hands around her hips, lifting her easily off the cart. The now familiar heat shot through her and she gasped.

He settled her gently on the ground, although he didn't immediately release her. For a brief second, his green eyes settled on her lips while a bemused expression blanketed his face. But then he shook his head as if to dismiss her from his mind.

Griogair handed the reins of one of the horse to Rory. "I left Duncan's horse still tethered to the tree."

"Guid," Rory said, taking the reins. He tilted his head to the pink sky. "He should have left the castle by now, and will likely be retrieving his mount soon."

He pivoted, and without saying another word, he lifted her up and settled her atop his horse. In the next moment, he mounted quickly behind her and urged the beast forward. She scarcely had enough time to hold on when the sound of hooves thundered in her ears.

They rode at a gallop, leaving everything familiar behind. The forest on either side of them became a blur of green. She prayed that Duncan had left her mother and Fyfa unharmed. She also prayed for an opportunity to escape from her captors.

They continued at a breakneck speed for a long while. But then Rory shouted to Griogair, and they slowed their horses down to an amble.

Rory relaxed his grasp on the reins, releasing one hand to rest it at her hip. While she should have brushed his hand aside, she felt his touch strangely pleasant and comforting.

Darra winced inwardly at the absurdity. This was not a good idea to become too comfortable with her captor. Moving away from him as much as she could, she allowed the cool autumn air to pass between them.

***

Rory shifted behind Darra, aware that a part of him was inconveniently awake, and rearing for action.

It was foolish to be lusting after the lass, he told himself sternly. She was English of all things. Still, it was difficult to ignore the temptress who sat directly in front of him. And with each inhalation, he caught the heady scent of roses and sandalwood. The women from the hills used plain soap and water, but Darra's perfume was exotic and teased his senses. Was her skin equally scented?

Her hair, which was the color of sun bleached straw, hung down her graceful back. When he saw her last night, he wasn't able to clearly observe her features. But now he saw too much of it, and he wished that the darkness once again concealed her visage. Yet he knew that he had to merely close his eyes, and a picture of her smooth oval face would come to mind.

A moment before, she rested her head against his shoulder. Every breath she took felt like his own. The lass was tired enough that she didn't realize that she sagged against him. Not that he minded. It had been too long since he bedded a woman, and the feel of Darra's soft body nestled against him felt pleasant. He shook his head, irritated with where his thoughts were leading him.

"Will ye stop moving?" he demanded.

Her spine stiffened. "'Tis not as if I have much space to begin with."

He snapped his mouth shut. When he allowed the lass to ride with him, he didn't consider that she would put him in a constant state of arousal. It was now that he regretted taking Darra with him rather than her mother.

"Why have you come to England to obtain a healer?" she asked. "Are there none in Scotland?"

Rory let out a long suffering sigh. He didn't want to converse with her, but she needed to know the details of his mission.

"Your mother was correct. Eanruing MacGregon is ill, and the village healer couldnae help him."

Even now, in his mind's eye, Rory could clearly see his father lying on his bed, his strength diminishing as each day passed.

Eanruing had been like this for many days with no sign of his fever abating. Slick sweat had beaded on his forehead, and his skin was pale and sickly.

"What can be done for him, Agnes?" Rory had asked the village healer, his tone low and guarded.

She assessed him with her dark, serious eyes. Agnes was a petite woman that was well past her prime. She lived in the village, and came as soon as he had sent for her. When his father first fell ill, he refused assistance, telling Rory and everyone else that he was all right, that he had survived worst illnesses. And Rory believed him. Except this time, Eanruing's sickness continued for many weeks. Then in the last few days, the fever started, and his health declined even further.

A ray of afternoon light broke through the window, and cast a thin strand of light onto the stone floor. All six of his siblings crowded around the bed — Duncan, Griogair, Cailean, Ewan, and his two sisters Mairead and Kila. His friend Blane Cunningtoun, who fostered at Tancraig Castle, and who was like a brother to him, was there as well. Without looking at them, Rory knew that various emotions flitted across their features. There was no need to speak since each of them recognized that Eanruing was fighting for his life.

Agnes wrung the cloth in the basin and slowly shook her head. "I cannae say for certain, Rory," she said. "However our clan willnae have anything tae fear as we now have ye as our Chief."

Chief. The address pierced through him like an arrow to his gut. He was no longer the Tanist but was the rightfully appointed Chief of Clan MacGregon. Only weeks before Eanruing decided to pass the clan responsibilities on to Rory.

One of his sisters, possibly Kila, let out a low moan of distress. Meanwhile Blane stared at him, his expression unreadable in the dim light.

"Can ye cure him, aye or nay?" Rory said, an impatient tic starting at his jaw. "Answer the question, Agnes."

She wiped her damp fingers on her apron, still avoiding his eyes. "Ye should have sent for me sooner."

"'Tis too late tae reflect on what I should have done." Anger began to simmer in his chest. However the vexation was directed at himself — for indulging his father. "Tell me what else ye can do for him."

"Wait," she nodded, her lips tightening into a grim line. "That's all that ye can do."

The sympathetic noise that Darra made drew Rory out of his dark musings.

"I'm sorry, what did ye say?" he asked.

"Was there nothing that the village healer could do for your father?" she repeated.

"Nay, she said that Eanruing was cursed, but I dinnae believe her blether," he paused. "'Tis the reason why we need tae obtain a real healer."

Chapter 5

ॐॐ

The dull light squeezed through the closed shutters, allowing just enough illumination for Venora to take full assessment of her bed chamber. The MacGregon spawn had left hours ago, and she was tied to a chair, a strip of cloth secured over her mouth. She had tried countless times to scream after the abominable Highlander had left, but the cloth around her mouth effectively muffled any sound that she made. That and it sucked all moisture from her mouth. Fear and worry swirled within her as she suffered in tortured silence. But there was also fury surging in her veins. After what the MacGregons did to her family, they dared to steal into her home, and insist on her help?

Venora glanced over at Fyfa. Somehow the maid had fallen asleep even though she was similarly bound to a chair. There was no way that *she* could have slept through all this.

She cast her eyes heavenward. *Forgive me, Arthur,* she pleaded silently. She should have gone with the Highlanders instead of letting them take Darra. At least if Venora went with them, she would have ended her miserable life, and be with her beloved. She blinked rapidly, shamed by her display of cowardice.

Her scrutiny fell upon the four-poster bed that sat off to the side of the chamber. It was the last place where Arthur had lain. She felt the familiar pang twisting in her chest, and a renewed sense of sorrow stabbed at her heart. She was a healer with a reputation for providing miracles. But in the end she couldn't save her own husband.

The image of Arthur lying in his bed floated to her consciousness, his pale face taut with pain and agony. All the things she had learned as a healer were useless. She squeezed her eyes shut, hoping to remove the image from her mind, but the picture remained as stark and real as if the nightmare was reoccurring.

"Here, love, take another sip of this tincture."

Venora had brought the cup to his mouth, but he lifted his hand, blocking it. The liquid sloshed, sliding down his chin, and gathering at the hollow of his neck.

"Arthur!" she cried, unable to contain the frustrated sob from her voice. This was her third attempt to administer the medication to him. She hurriedly grabbed a cloth from the side table and dabbed at the spilled medicine.

"I am sorry," he said, giving her a tired though charming smile. It was a smile that had won her over when they first met, and any anger she felt dissipated. Arthur reached over and placed his hand on hers, the firm weight of it stilling her movements. He licked his lips as if he wanted to say something.

"What is it?" she whispered, bending down to hear him.

"Death awaits, sweeting," he said, his voice faint. "You cannot help me."

She drew back in alarm. "Nay, my lord! Do not tell me this! You must drink this tincture that I have made. You will get well, you will see." But even as she said this, doubts were creeping into her mind. The injuries that her husband sustained in his limbs were deep. He refused to die in the battlefield, and insisted that he return to Lancullin Castle. By the time he arrived, his body was depleted from the loss of blood, and the festering wounds in his legs.

Venora tried her best to clean the cuts, but the next day tiny red streaks appeared on his pale skin. His breath came out in short pants, as if he struggled for air, and his heart slowed, beating faintly in his chest. Out of desperation, she summoned the village hag to chase away the Angel of Death. The witch arrived and immediately began to chant invocations, her incoherent words resounding in the chamber for long hours.

"The grip of death on my lord is too much," the old woman gasped. "I cannot do anything more for Sir Arthur. He will be dead within a day."

"Nay," Venora said, shaking her head slowly. "You are lying."

And she truly believed it. The servants cast sympathetic looks at her, their expressions showing that they sided with the hag. But Venora was determined to prove that everyone was wrong. After all, she came from a line of great healers, and the healing arts flowed in her veins. Didn't the hundreds of people she helped in the past attest to her abilities?

"Get out!" she shouted to everyone in the chamber. Then she glared at the witch. "You are of no use to me."

One by one, the people filed out of the chamber, and she was left alone with Arthur. She moved to the side table to prepare another herbal concoction.

"She was only trying to help," Arthur said from his bed, his voice weak.

"Nay 'twas a mistake to bring that woman here." She swiveled around, and gulped back a lump in her throat when she saw his pale, wane visage. Moving closer to him, she said, "Here, try this, my lord. I know it tastes bitter, but it will make you feel better."

A ghost of a smile flitted across his firm lips. He lifted his hand and placed his palm on the side of her cheek. "Having you here by my side is all that I need to make me feel better," he said.

She set the cup down on the table and raised her hands to cover his. Closing her eyes, she felt the tears burn beneath her eyelids.

"I am sorry that I cannot heal you from your suffering." She dashed away at a tear that slipped down her cheek.

His gaze shifted to the ceiling, his eyes appearing unfocused. "'Tis God's will —"

"You mean to leave me," she choked out. "I — I do not know how I can go on…"

"Venora," he said.

When she met his gaze, she saw sorrow and regret reflected in his depths. "My time is nigh, but you — you need to be strong … for Darra…"

She gripped his hand more tightly as if she could pour her own life force into him, and keep him alive. But even as she held his hand, his strength began to fade. More tears fell, and she lifted her other hand to wipe them away. When her vision cleared, she saw that Arthur had fallen asleep. The lines of pain had smoothed away from his handsome face, and for once he seemed at peace.

Reluctantly she took his hand away from her cheek and placed it gently at his side.

She reached over to adjust the blanket when she hesitated. The steady rise and fall of his chest was strangely absent. Her heart skipped a beat. Hoping that it was merely her imagination, she quickly reached to feel the pulse at the side of his neck.

Nothing.

She staggered back, horror gripping her heart.

"Nay," she whispered brokenly. Then a wailing filled the chamber, the sound as desperate and pain-filled as an animal dying in the woods.

As if a dam had broken, tears flooded down her cheeks. And all the sorrow that she held at bay burst forth with a fury that left her breathless and weak.

In the end, the witch's prophecy came true. The tincture that Venora made only helped to dull his pain and allow him to die in peace. Even though she denied it at the time, she knew that truthfully, there was nothing she could have done for him. And there was nothing that she could do to bring him back to life. And even though Arthur had insisted that she stay strong, she couldn't do it. Venora fell into fit of despair, and through a twist of fate, Darra was the one who became the pillar of strength.

With great effort, Venora tried to rebury her sorrow, but it burst through anyway. The hot tears burned down her cheeks while her heart wrenched in pain. However all her sufferings were muffled by the cloth barrier biting into her mouth.

For too long she had wallowed in her grief and was consumed by helplessness. And in her shortcoming, she permitted her sole child to be taken away by Scottish savages.

A noise at the door drew her attention, dragging her out from her terrible musings. She glanced over at Fyfa. The maid was awake and staring intently at the door.

The door creaked open.

"Oh!" a voice gasped. The urn that the young servant held in her hand tipped over to the side. The water splashed onto the floor, while the blood drained from the girl's cheeks. She stared at Venora as if she was an apparition.

"Get me out of here!" Venora yelled. But the sound that emerged from her covered mouth seemed as if she screamed underwater.

Still, the girl understood what it was that Venora wanted. She set the urn on the floor, and rushed over to free them from their prisons.

"Why are you tied, milady?"

She shook her head impatiently, not wanting to discuss what had happened. Time was running out, and she needed to get to Darra.

"Get Sir Jarin," she ordered.

"Aye, milady," the girl said, giving her a clumsy curtsy before dashing out of the bed chamber.

She didn't have to wait long before she heard the heavy ring of boots running rapidly across the corridor. In the next moment, her loyal commander burst into the chamber.

"Milady!" he said, panting. "I came as quickly as I could." His dark eyes scanned all around, taking in her disheveled appearance, the broadsword on the other side of the chamber, and the pile of rope gathered near the chairs.

One black brow raised, and before he had a chance to ask, Venora spoke. "My daughter has been kidnapped last night, and we need to get her back."

"Last night?" A stunned look appeared on his countenance, but he recovered from his shock. "Do you know where the captors are taking her?"

"Aye," she drew in a deep breath. "To the highlands."

"I am not familiar with the highlands, milady, but I will gather my men and track her down." He turned to leave.

"Sir Jarin," she said, stopping him. "I will be joining you."

"But milady, you are —"

She shook her head impatiently. "I know exactly where they are taking her."

***

Venora and her small troop cleared the drawbridge just when a group of six men rode toward them. The standard waving in the air was unmistakable.

"Why, 'tis Sir Dudley," he said, turning to her in surprise.

A ball of dread churned in her stomach. Of all things, the neighboring knight was the last person that she wanted to encounter today.

Dudley halted before them. He surveyed the castle behind her, and then directed his narrowed gaze at her riding party. His keen eyes glittered with suspicion.

"I have come to visit Lady Darra," he said. He pulled his reins to still the horse while his men waited silently behind him. There was no mistaking who held the authority in this group. The knight was dressed in a dark blue tunic that was rich and velvety. The color of his clothes complemented his hair, which was dark and shot with silver strands. The hose he wore clung to his wiry legs. He was a slim man a few years older than Venora's forty summers. The cloak draped over his shoulders gave him the illusion of bulk. But it wasn't his appearance that caused men and women to cringe. It was the incredible meanness that shone in his dark pupils. This trait was something that Venora noted in Dudley since the first time they met. When gossip reached her ears about the lord, she was riveted and horrified about what she had learned. And when the knight began to show interest in Darra, she became nervous. Arthur was in discussion about a possible marriage between Dudley and their daughter. She realized that they needed to fulfill their obligation, and find a suitable husband for Darra. But even though Dudley had wealth and influence, Venora couldn't allow the match to occur.

"He is a terrible man!" she told Arthur.

"All warriors have a fierceness about them," he said, frowning.

"Nay," she shook her head with vehemence. "'Tis something more. You already know that his first wife died at childbirth. The second one died of some mysterious cause." She searched his eyes, willing that he saw the seriousness of her concern. "And the third wife, who was the same age as Darra, died as well. There are speculations that Sir Dudley was cruel toward her, and she ended her life to escape from him."

Arthur watched her silently, and she felt compelled to press forward. "I love my daughter too much to allow her to suffer under the hands of a vicious lord. And — and I believe that you feel the same."

"Fine," he said, letting out a long sigh. "I will speak with him once I return from battle."

Unfortunately Arthur never had a chance to speak to Dudley. It was a few days after the funeral that the knight arrived, insisting on his claim to marry Darra. Venora sent him away at that time, but here he was again. She had run out of excuses and was uncertain how much longer she could discourage him from her daughter.

"You will need to come at another time," she said, her voice trembling slightly. The horse underneath her detected her fear and reared slightly.

Jarin reached over, and grabbed her reins to settle the nervous horse. She offered a grateful smile to the garrison commander. But Jarin wasn't looking at her. He was staring at Dudley, his expression steely. She took in a fortifying breath, knowing that he would protect her with his life.

She gave her horse a reassuring pat at the side of its neck. Clearing her throat, she spoke again, only this time her voice was much stronger. "My daughter is not receiving visitors this day."

"I have traveled a distance to see Lady Darra," he said, clearly not liking her answer. Dudley's pupils were beady and hard, watching her as if he was a spider, and she was a fly that hovered too close to his web. If Jarin was not at her side, it was likely that he would have forced his way into Lancullin Castle.

"You would spurn me again, milady?" Dudley asked, his voice softening, although she detected an underlining threat behind his question.

She swallowed, and resisted the urge to dig her heels into the horse's side, and plow past the troop that blocked her.

Despite holding much clout with the king, she doubted that Arthur would have allowed Dudley to intimidate him. And so no matter how difficult it was, she couldn't allow the knight to scare her either.

"As I have said, my daughter cannot see you today." She wiped a sweaty palm on her gown. "I have business to attend. Move aside, sire, or I will have my guards move you by force."

He stroked his chin and frowned, the gestures making him appear unfriendly and conniving. It seemed as if he was used to having his way, and he didn't appreciate a mere woman ordering him about.

She glanced over at Jarin and his men. But the garrison commander and the two guards that accompanied them fixed their stares on the opposing knights. The guards at the gates and along the battlements also stood at attention. With one bellow, Jarin had the ability to hail the entire garrison to join him. And Dudley was cognizant of this.

"This is a rather rude reception, milady." His eyes constricted to tiny dots as they leveled on her. "'Tis my belief that the business you need to attend is right in front of you." His fists gripped onto his reins, the whites of his knuckles showing. When he spoke again, there was venom behind his words. "I had an understanding with your late husband. This matter is not finished, milady." He paused, his eyes narrowing at her. "I am not a patient man, and mean to claim my bride."

A maternal instinct filled her, and she straightened her shoulders. It was true that she was a woman, but that didn't mean that he would frighten her into submission. "You do *not* have a claim over my daughter," she said, her voice frigid. "My husband was to tell you that your suit was declined, except he never had the chance."

A skeptical expression crossed over Dudley's face. He urged his horse closer to her and leaned in; he was so close that she could smell his rancid breath. Dropping his voice so only she could hear, he said, "Why is it that I do not believe you, milady?" His lips curled downward. "You can claim that your dead husband was going to deny my suit, but there is no proof. And he cannot speak from the grave, now can he?" He leaned back abruptly. "The king will hear about this affair," he said.

A chill streaked down her spine. It had never occurred to her that Dudley would use his influence with the king to have his way. Subsequently if King Harold became involved, she would have no choice but to allow the marriage.

"Milady," Jarin said, sidling his horse next to hers. He frowned at the sight of the other knight's hands on her reins. "We will leave now."

Dudley glared sharply at the commander. Jarin was a younger, fitter knight, and Dudley had a cause to be cautious.

One of Dudley's men advanced, his hand on the hilt of his broadsword. But he stayed the guard.

"We will discuss this later," he said, his lips stretching across his slim face, although the smile didn't quite reach his eyes.

He was letting her off easily, she realized. Slowly, she released the air that she was holding.

"Aye, later," she repeated, wanting to end the conversation. "Sir Jarin, let us leave."

But later came much too soon. Venora had asked her men to stop so that she could attend to her needs. It should have been a simple stop, but when she emerged from the woods, she saw that Dudley held her commander at knifepoint. The other two guards were surrounded. She turned back to the thicket, intending to flee, however one of Dudley's men chased her down, and dragged her back to the small clearing.

"Where is Lady Darra?" Dudley demanded.

Jarin strained against the men who held him. "Let go of milady!"

Dudley sneered at the garrison commander before showing him his back.

"You have not answered my question, milady," he said, his features as hard as granite.

"I do not know what you are talking about," she said tightly. "I already told you that my daughter is ill…"

"Do not take me for a fool." His beady eyes bore down on her. "I know that you would not venture out on your own without good reason. Tell me where she is," his gaze flicked over to Jarin, "Or your favorite knight dies."

The air seized in her lungs.

"Do not kill him!" she burst out. Then it immediately occurred to her that Dudley might be useful in her scheme to retrieve Darra from the MacGregons. She took a deep breath. "Darra has been taken by the Scots. That is why we have left Lancullin Castle — to get her back."

"Another lie!" Dudley yelled.

"Nay! 'Tis the truth. The Highlanders broke into my chamber intending to kidnap me, but they took Darra instead."

He leaned back on his horse, studying her. Then he spit on the ground. "I will accompany you, and will bring back what is mine."

His face was flushed, and she perceived the one thing that Dudley hated most were the Scots. He was well aware that she was a Scotswoman, yet he tolerated her because she styled herself after the English, and was married to an influential lord. If Dudley ever found out what she intended, he would despise her, and maybe even kill her. But that was a risk she had to take. She would save Darra, and not fail her like she failed her husband.

Chapter 6

ॐ∽ॐ

"'Tis the reason why we need tae obtain a real healer." Rory's last words echoed in Darra's mind. She was a healer, and ignoring the sick was not what one did. But then again, not many healers were kidnapped, and forced to treat someone.

A gust of wind blew, and caused gooseflesh to prickle across her forearms. She rubbed at her arms in an attempt to warm herself.

Darra straightened up in her seated position and bumped against his firm chest. The chill momentarily was forgotten as she felt a tingle of heat in the area that touched him.

Groping for some topic to distract herself, she spoke the first thing that came to mind. "Why were you so intent in bringing my mother with you?"

"'Tis apparent that my da is acquainted with Lady Venora," Rory said. "In his delirium, he called out her name. The village healer recalled that long ago your mother's kin assisted Clan MacGregon with a matter of health."

"My mother has never spoken of it," she said, surprised.

"Well, I have never heard of —" He broke off, and pulled the reins so that the horse came to a complete stop.

Griogair halted next to him. "What is it?" he asked.

"The ground is disturbed." Rory pointed to a mud filled groove at the side of the dirt road.

She leaned forward, trying to get a better glimpse at the ground. It had rained the night before, and if a transport had come through this way, then it wasn't unusual for it to make dents in the mud.

"'Tis nothing more than the wheel marks made by a farmer's cart," Griogair said.

Rory dismounted and approached the spot. Crouching down, he inspected the area while a sense of foreboding started to envelop him. The grooves in the drying mud seemed unnatural, like a heavy device was dragged through it. Something shiny reflected in the mud, and after closer examination, he discovered a metal object jutting out from the silt. With trepidation continuing to creep up his back, he reached for the object.

"'Twas nae a farmer's cart." He stood up and held the object in the air. "Nay farmer owns one of these."

"A gauntlet?" Darra asked, surprised.

Griogair shook his head in disbelief. "Do ye think some rogue knights have passed through here?" he asked.

"Nay," he tossed the offending object into the bushes. "'Tis likely that they're Harold's men."

"Harold's men," Griogair repeated and leaned back on his horse. "We fought them back two months earlier…"

"Aye, and we'll continue tae fight them until they leave us in peace," he said grimly. "We'll find a place tae stop and wait for Duncan tae catch up with us." He walked over to the nearby bushes, plucked off a broad leaf and began to wipe the mud from his fingers. "We dinnae want tae come across the cavalry by accident. From the track marks on the ground, I would say that they're a few hours ahead of us."

"Or they could be stationed nearby," Griogair pointed out. "Do ye think they have plans tae raid Scotland again?"

"'Tis probable." He tossed the leaf onto the ground. Looking over at his brother, he asked, "How much further do we have till we reach the border?"

Griogair carelessly slapped at a mosquito on his neck before reaching into his leather sporran and producing a map. He carefully unfolded the parchment, and began to study it. Silent for a long while, he traced a forefinger along the chart. Finally, he lifted his head.

"If we continue without stopping," he said, his brows creasing in concentration, "I estimate that we'll make it tae the border within half a day."

Rory frowned and examined Darra. Exhaustion was clearly etched on her countenance. "'Twould nae be guid if we stumbled upon the enemy camp while we're fatigued. Those savages," he spat forcefully onto the ground, "traverse with the devil himself, and wouldnae hesitate tae slay us if they came upon our party."

Darra raised her chin and looked down her nose at him. "The English are *not* savages," she said fiercely.

"But ye are savages of the worst kind," he said dismissively. "Just ask the poor widows who lost their husbands, or the women who were raped by your sae called noble knights."

She fell silent.

"See?" his lips tightened into a thin line. "Ye ken there is truth in what I say."

"There is no truth," she said, inhaling swiftly through her nose. "You cannot judge an entire people by the actions of a few dishonorable men."

As he walked toward her, her grip on the reins tightened as if she was ready to spur the beast into a gallop. Rory caught Griogair's eye, and his brother acknowledged his warning without a word passing between them.

The lass spun her head around in time to catch their exchange. Her hold on the reins loosened, as if she registered that if she tried to escape, Griogair would be upon her faster than a falcon picking out its prey.

Rory mounted the horse and settled behind her before she could entertain further ideas. But her words disturbed him and he pondered them until he dismissed them altogether. The English were all untrustworthy as far as he was concerned. Once Darra was finished with healing Eanruing, then he could be rid of her.

***

Rory shifted his eyes eastward, scanning the thick line of trees that surrounded them. Large moss covered boulders continually blocked their path, and they were forced to travel in single file in order to maneuver around the obstacles. And as the light within the forest faded, they were compelled to move even slower through the tangled undergrowth. The last thing he needed was to have one of the horses slip and injure itself. Even though he preferred to travel at a faster clip, he sensed that he needed to move with more caution.

And much as he loathed to do it, he also had to account for the well-being of the lass. It would have been easier if he stuck to the original mission, and took Lady Venora with him. From what he understood, the Lady of Lancullin was a Scotswoman, and she would be familiar with the rough terrain. But instead, Rory had taken her daughter, a fragile English woman born and bred.

He was also aware that he would confront difficult, and unpleasant questions when he returned to the highlands with the lass. Rory had already encountered opposition when he told his kin about his initial plans.

"Ye dinnae mean tae bring Lady Venora here do ye?" Duncan had said, his voice tight with disapproval.

"Aye, I cannae believe that bringing the English woman here will help Eanruing," Blane joined in, spitting on the ground as if to emphasize his words.

"She isnae really English," Rory said grimly. While the men surrounded him, he calmly looked at each one. "Besides, we have nay choice. The village healer disnae ken what else tae do. And if this lady is as renowned as they say, then she'll be able tae cure Da."

His brothers looked at him, their faces unconvinced.

"I dinnae think that we can trust Lady Venora," Duncan said. He shook his head while anger and hatred seeped into his voice. "Even if she isnae English, she still lives among the bastards."

"It disnae matter where she lives," Rory said tightly.

"I agree with Duncan," Blane interjected, his face stony. "By marrying an English lord this woman has turned her back on us, her countrymen. I'll have nothing tae do with her."

"Ye can help me bring her here or nae. I willnae force ye," he scowled at Duncan and Blane. "But ken this. I intend tae bring the healer back with me. I owe Da at least this much."

"I still dinnae think this is a guid idea," Duncan said, scowling back. "'Tis the devil's domain that we'll be entering. Dinnae ye remember the destruction and bloodshed that the English knights caused us in the last battle? Tae this day the bastards plot tae cross our borders, and steal what is rightfully ours."

"Aye," Griogair agreed. "We have already lost many men tae the greedy whoresons."

"Those men couldnae be saved," Rory said more harshly than he intended.

His gut wrenched with pain and torment over the senseless massacre of men who fought for Gertrude, Queen of Scots. For centuries, the kings of England had placed their focus on bonny Scotland, and when King Harold came to rule, he was no different. In fact, he was more ruthless with his greed and ambitions than his predecessors.

When Harold decided to attack Scotland, Gertrude put a call to all clans to unite. Suddenly petty wars between the many clans ceased.

As Clan Chief at the time, Eanruing was adamant in sending help to Gertrude. Rory had no qualms about driving out the English scum. But he did have reservations over supporting a weak queen who favored dancing and festivities over the welfare of her people. But as Tanist, heir to the chiefdom, he had no choice but to follow the dictates of his father, and lead his clan to war.

And while Rory wasn't the one to butcher his kin, he ignored his instincts to retreat, which resulted in the deaths of many of his clansmen. But his gut told him that Eanruing's life could be saved. This time he would listen.

"If we dinnae act on this, we'll lose Da as well," he said, compressing his lips into a firm line. "I'll leave now. Ye can come with me or nae."

A silence fell over the group.

"I'll go," Griogair said, stepping forward.

Duncan let out a sigh. "Though I think 'tis a foolish idea, I'll go too."

"Well I cannae go," Blane said, his features twisted in anger at the very idea. "I cannae stand tae be near the scum who killed my friends," his voice cracked with emotion, and he swallowed audibly, "and my family."

Rory nodded. "Ye can stay then."

"What do ye propose that we do?" Griogair asked quietly.

"Aye, what's your plan, Rory?" Duncan said, studying his face.

"I will appeal tae her as a Scot. A true Scotswoman will find it within her heart tae assist our plight. It will take us two days tae cross the border, and another day tae reach Lancullin Castle. Then the task of bringing her here should be simple enough."

Unfortunately, the mission wasn't easy at all.

He rolled back his shoulders, trying to loosen the tension that settled there. The act provided no relief. That weight sat on Rory shoulders ever since Eanruing fell ill, and he took over as the new Chief of Clan MacGregon.

"'Tis far enough, dinnae ye think, Rory?" Griogair asked, interrupting Rory's heavy thoughts.

The lass who was almost dozing became alert.

Rory shook his head. The pondering of war and clan government would have to wait. Right now he needed to focus on getting them home safely. And that meant sneaking past the English cavalry and bypassing the hostile Scottish clans along the way.

Up ahead the forest was already in shadows. If they didn't set up camp soon, they would be hard pressed to see anything past their noses.

He turned to stare in the direction in which they had come. The sound of rushing water was much louder here. The wind was starting to pick up as well, causing the leaves to rustle in the tree tops.

"Aye," he said, stopping his horse. They were far enough from the main road that their cooking fire wouldn't be detected. Duncan would also have no trouble finding them. "We'll halt at this spot."

They dismounted and Griogair went to tether the horses to a nearby tree.

His brother pulled off a sack of oats from one of the horses and fed the beasts. Meanwhile Rory grabbed the sack that contained all of their provisions and cooking tools. They had brought just enough food to allow them to cross over the border and back.

He glanced toward the river, and the idea of eating fresh fish made his stomach rumble.

"Griogair," he said. His brother looked up from his task. "When ye are done with that, go tae the river and catch us some fish tae eat."

"And me?" Darra asked. "What will you have me do?"

Rory looked at her, startled by her question. "Ye will sit on that rock, lass."

"I have done nothing but sit all day," she said, frowning.

Something in the tone of her voice made him soften slightly. She was the first English noblewoman that he had met, and it surprised him that she wanted to perform menial chores. He shrugged, seeing no harm in letting her help him. Rummaging through the sack, he pulled out a small pot.

"Ye can fetch some water for cooking," he said, beckoning her to follow him.

They walked in silence, although the roar of rushing water could be heard even before they reached the river bank.

Behind him, darkness had engulfed the thicket, while over the watercourse, the sun was only beginning to set over the trees. Numerous rocks of varying sizes scattered along the bank and within the rushing river itself.

Birds called from the trees tops, their voices alerting other critters that there were foreigners in their midst.

An alder tree which grew right at the river's edge was damaged by the previous night's storm. A bolt of lightning had stuck it, and it leaned gracefully over the currents.

"Here, use this," he said, handing her the small pot. "I'll be over there searching for wood."

Darra took the pot and walked to the river's edge. She stood there, scanning her surroundings with the bleak realization that she had no idea where she was. Turning her head, she saw that Rory was busy gathering wood. But then he bent over, his form unexpectedly disappearing behind the shrubs.

Her lips twisted with the irony of it. Here was her one chance to flee, but there was nowhere to run. She could go up or down river, but then what? She couldn't run aimlessly through the forest. Another idea was to cross over the river. But she struck that notion down since she wasn't an experienced swimmer, and the river currents appeared treacherous.

She let out a frustrated sigh. Her best option was to get the pot of water as Rory had asked. Last night's storm had caused the banks to become soft and muddy. In order to get to the water that was less murky, she had to traverse over the boggy slope. However she loathed the thought of getting her slippers or any part of her dirty. But how could she to get to the water without touching the sludge?

Looking up, she assessed the splintered tree that leaned over the river. Her eyes followed the length of the bole, and she noticed that it braced against a large rock. Except for the damage to the trunk itself, it was still attached to the base of the tree. From her angle, the log seemed sturdy enough to support her weight. If she went on it with bare feet, she would have a better grip on the tree limb. In the end, she could solve two problems at once — avoid getting her shoes soiled, and scoop up clean water for cooking. Aye, she would complete the task, and lull Rory into letting down his guard. When the next opportunity arose, she would be ready to take it.

With that resolve, she took off her slippers and climbed onto the broken tree. Grabbing a hold of the bough beside her, she inched her way closer toward the center of the log. The roar of the river seemed much louder here, while the wind whipped her hair across her face.

The water below her feet hurtled against the rock, causing an icy spray to spatter her. She paused and bit her lip in concentration. Without meaning to, she peeked down at the vigorous currents that churned and bubbled beneath her.

She could die at any moment, she thought wildly. This would be her ultimate means for escape, except she didn't want to perish. Her nails dug into the tree limb while she stood frozen in one spot, her heart trapped in her gullet. Even as the cold, wet air lashed around her, she was conscious of the sweat that beaded on her forehead and that ran down her back. This was not a good plan, and she needed to retreat.

Her grip on the branch tightened even more, as she pulled on it; she had every intention to get back to solid ground. But her desperate purchase on the branch caused it to snap, throwing her off balance.

A scream tore from her lips as she fell down, down, down.

The impact of the freezing water immediately cut off her scream, and stung her eyes. She was forced to shut them just as the murky water closed over her. But as quickly as she plunged into the raging water, the current hauled her back to the top. Darra burst through the surface, gulping a lungful of air before coughing and sputtering. She had only enough time to gasp another breath of air when she was pulled under again.

Flinging her hands out, she blindly, frantically searched for something concrete to anchor her. Somehow her fingers brushed against some leaves, and she instinctively latched onto them. Then with strength that she didn't know she possessed, she yanked herself up until she broke through the surface again. The water sprayed in every direction.

"Help!" she cried, praying that Rory would hear her. But any chance of being heard was drowned out by the thundering water flow.

Chapter 7

Rory picked up a piece of wood. He twisted it around in his hand, inspecting the moss covered branch before tossing it aside. It was impossible to find decent kindling since last night's storm made everything damp.

He started toward the small overhang that was off to his right. That area at least didn't seem as wet, and there was a possibility that he might find dry wood there. When he bent down to pick up another piece of kindling, he heard something odd, something that sounded almost like a scream. It was likely some wild animal screeching in the thicket, but for some inexplicable reason, the hairs at the back of his neck rose. He heard it again, and this time there was no mistaking the clamor of someone in distress, someone who was Darra.

Rory had been more lax with Darra since he was certain that she had no means of escape, but now he cursed himself for allowing her out of his sight. Truly he couldn't see how she would have gotten herself into trouble. All he asked her to do was to fetch some water.

It wasn't a difficult task, and it benefited her as well as everyone else.

Dropping the stack of wood that he carried onto the ground, he looked around him. Obviously, the forest was teeming with various animals. Since she was a skittish lass, perhaps some wee beastie had frightened her.

But she was nowhere to be seen. He crashed through the shrubbery, and looked over to where he last saw her. Perhaps she was fooling with him, and would emerge from her hiding place soon. However his hope vanished as soon as he caught sight of a pair of small leather slippers that sat neatly next to a storm ravaged tree trunk. The damage to the tree was extensive. Lightning had stuck it straight through, and the entire trunk leaned precariously into the rapid flowing river.

He could feel his heart accelerating even though the sound was almost drowned out by the noise from the river. Racing over to the river's edge, he pulled aside the nearby shrubs and peered down into the cloudy water. The fierce wind ripped up the currents, pulling broken branches and other debris along as if they competed in some sort of contest.

Did she fall in?

"Darra!" he yelled, trying to make himself heard over the surging water.

He shoved aside the bushes, and caught sight of her, clinging desperately on to a tree branch that dangled in the water.

"Dinnae move!" he shouted. Even from this distance, he could sense her heartrending fear. And he realized that if he didn't get to her in time, she would be swept away. "I'm coming tae get ye, lass!"

In his haste, his foot caught in a tangle of roots, and before he could free himself, his worst fear came true. The branch that she clutched made a sickening crack, snapping into two. The river took her away, its greedy waves swallowing her up.

"Nay!" He scrambled down the muddy bank, slipping and sliding in his rush to get to her. Suddenly it seemed all too certain that death hovered nearby. Although he didn't want to admit it, he was starting to like the wee hellion, and he definitely didn't want to see her killed.

***

Darra yanked hard on the tree branch, fighting to break through to the surface of the water so she could breathe. But it was too much for the branch to both support her weight and resist the strong current. And when the tree limb snapped, she was dragged back in; the water carried her away, pushing her through its turbid depths.

Even with fear choking her, her body managed to avoid crashing into the obstacles and debris in her path. Her skin was raw from scraping against the jagged rocks, although that was the least of her worries. She was getting tired, and she recognized that in order to survive, she needed to somehow overcome her exhaustion. However this proved to be a difficult task. The turbulent water rippled around her, and pulled her under time and again.

Please God, I do not want to die! She squeezed her eyes shut in a desperate prayer.

She let out a small whimper when another wave crashed over her head, making her sputter.

But just when she was about to surrender all hope, she caught sight of an object sticking out of the water. Allowing the river flow to drive her closer, she saw that it was a tree that was wrecked by the storm. It was as if God had answered her prayers. The lightning had split the tree, although a large section of it was still attached to a trunk which stood firm along the river bank.

Darra started to swim toward it, using the last of her strength. If she didn't make it to the log, she was doomed. But she couldn't think of that now. Pushing forward, she kicked her legs and swam hard in the direction of the broken tree. Once she was in line with the log, she allowed the current to propel her to the target. It was coming closer and closer. Then she grabbed one of the branches and held on tight.

The freezing water made her teeth clatter, and she started to fight with exhaustion again. Instinctively she saw that she could reach safety if only she could heave herself onto the broken tree.

"Move closer tae me!" a voice shouted, above the punishing water.

She looked up, half thinking that she was dreaming. But Rory's familiar countenance filled her vision, and hope flooded to her chest. He was on the river bed, stretching out his hand for her to grab. But a gap still existed between them. She either had to move closer to Rory, or he would have to come to her. It was a dangerous undertaking in either circumstance.

Darra gripped the log, afraid to let go. What if the river swept her away again? She was fatigued. The course ahead seemed even more riddled with sizable rocks. If she smashed into one of those boulders, she would likely be injured or killed.

"I cannot," she cried.

Then he did something that she didn't expect him to do. He took off his boots and came down the muddy bank. While holding tightly onto a branch attached to the damaged tree, he carefully maneuvered in her direction.

"Take my hand," he yelled.

She stared helplessly at his outstretched hand, although she was well aware that she couldn't stay in the water forever. Rory gave her an encouraging look. And this time, she decided to trust him. Putting out a trembling hand, she reached for him. His warm, strong grip enclosed over her wrist as he pulled her toward him.

"I will lift ye, but ye have tae grab the shrubbery and pull yourself up, understand?" he said.

"Aye," she said, giving a tired nod. She was shivering and her teeth clattered uncontrollably.

He hoisted her up so she could reach a shrub and drag herself onto dry land. Finally, she was safe, and her heart could cease its frantic pace.

A moment later Rory followed her, clambering onto the bank. He threw himself down beside her, his breath coming out in harsh spurts.

She glanced over at him. "Th — thank you," she said, barely able to get the word out.

"Ye gave me quite a fright," he said.

"I — I was fri — frightened as well," she said, hugging her arms to her chest, and rocking to and fro.

"Ye are shivering," he said, frowning. "Let me warm ye."

"But I will get you wet," she said.

Ignoring her protest, he picked her up as if she weighed no more than a flower petal, and placed her on his lap. Unpinning his brooch, he loosened the top section of his great kilt. He reached behind him, dragging the surplus fabric over his shoulders and wrapping it around them. His heavy arms then gathered her close, pressing her against his muscular chest.

"There, that should warm ye," he said.

Indeed, she felt the warmth emanating from his torso, although she was still cold. For too long, she was caught in the icy water, and the memory of it sent another shiver through her. She tucked her head underneath his chin, and his powerful arms tightened in response.

Rory held her like this for a long while, and she was grateful for it.

With her ear pressed to his chest, she could hear the solid, static beating of his heart. Except for her father, she had never sat this close to a man before. Snuggling against Rory, she breathed in his musky male scent. She was comforted by their intimacy, and for some peculiar reason, she felt content too. Perhaps the horrid ordeal had changed her, but it no longer mattered to her that Rory was a Scot, and that her people saw him as the enemy. All that mattered was that he cared enough to save her. And when he rescued her, he gave no thought to his own safety. Was this a sign of a callous savage who didn't have a heart?

She had never really examined Rory before, but now that he held her in his arms, she studied his rugged beauty. He seemed to belong to the wilderness since the air of untamed power enveloped him like a second skin, making him appear dangerous, ruthless. Unable to help it, his proximity caused her to shudder, but she knew it wasn't from fear or from the cold.

His tousled red hair fell slightly above his shoulders, framing a narrow, handsome visage. It was almost sinful that he should look so fair. But he seemed unaware or unconcerned about his physical attributes. At the moment, his forehead was creased with worry, and his beautiful green eyes were tempered by gentleness. She really didn't know what to make of his expression, since he declared that he despised everything English. Well, *she* was English; there was no disputing that fact. Still, his manner seemed to suggest that he liked her. Or at least liked her enough to see to her comfort.

Darra surveyed the curve of his strong jaw structure, and noticed that it was covered with crimson stubble. For some bizarre reason she wanted to skim her fingers along his jaw, and feel the bristly roughness there.

He was so different from any other man that she had known. In fact he was the polar opposite to Sir Dudley, her suitor. First of all, Rory was younger and more fair than the other knight. When Rory spoke to her, it was as if he saw her as a person and not chattel. And when he looked at her, she felt as desirable as one of the exquisite ladies at King Harold's court.

Sir Dudley, on the other hand, saw her as a sole means to breed his offspring. This wasn't an unusual concept. A woman of her stature could only hope to marry a kind, respectable lord. Except that when she became acquainted with Sir Dudley, she discovered that while he was respectable, he was not kind. He had proved his unpleasantness when he demanded that she honor an agreement that he had forged with her father.

"We had a pact," the old knight said. "A year ago, Sir Arthur pledged your daughter to me in marriage. I am now ready to marry her."

"Darra is not ready to marry yet," Lady Venora said, her face turning white.

"I understand that she is almost eighteen years old — an age that is ripe for marriage."

"My husband has recently died, sire," she said, blinking rapidly. She laced her fingers together and folded them on the trestle table. "I cannot allow Lady Darra to marry while we still grieve."

Darra caught her mother's eye and sent her a grateful look.

"Nevertheless the maiden will need a man to support her," he said, ignoring the exchange between mother and daughter. He sent Darra a leering smile. "And what better man to provide for her than an established lord like myself?"

A streak of fear ran through Darra, negating the relief that she experienced earlier. "We will need to consider my other marriage prospects as well, sire," she said, daring to voice the first thing that came to her mind.

Sir Dudley fingered the sleeve of his tunic as his eyes swept over her figure. She suppressed a shudder.

"My sources tell me that you have no other marriage prospects, my dear." Suddenly he thrust out his chest. "Fine, I owe that you are both grieving over the loss of a good knight. I will allow one year for you to overcome your grief. And milady," he said, giving Lady Venora a long measured look, "after this mourning period, I mean to take Lady Darra as wife."

His words sounded like a threat, and Darra glanced at her mother in alarm.

The knight pivoted and exited the great hall with his guards following in his wake.

But of course that situation occurred almost a year ago. They had gone back to their routine where Sir Dudley called upon her on occasion. Darra bore those visits with restrained civility, and was glad when he left her in peace.

In the meantime, she had thrown herself into her work, healing the castle inhabitants and the peasants that came to seek her help. Any free time she had, she spent in the solar brewing, and experimenting with new herbal formulations.

Darra sighed, forcibly dragging her mind back to the present. Rory's warmth seeped into her chilled body, and she relaxed against his firm trunk.

Why couldn't her suitor be more like this Highlander? A sudden inherent desire awakened in her, and her heart began to flutter at the thought of having his firm lips pressed against hers. What would it feel like? Tender. Passionate. Delicious. It would be all those things, she realized. And most of all it, would be different from the sloppy kisses that she received from Sir Dud —

"Ye are safe now," Rory said, his deep brogue interrupting her thoughts.

"Aye," she said, his words reminding her that she nearly drowned in the rapids. If he hadn't searched for her when she plummeted into the watercourse, she would likely be dead now. That notion caused a lump to form at the back of her throat.

"The current," she cleared her throat, and tried again, "The current was fierce, and it kept pulling me under, and — and I thought for certain that…"

"Dinnae think about it," he said softly. He placed his callused thumb and forefinger under her chin, tilting it up. "Ye are here with me now, do ye understand?"

She nodded and closed her eyes. The smooth cadence of his voice glided over her skin, soothing her nerves, comforting her. He dropped his hand and placed it lightly at her hip. She heard the concern in his voice, and it surprised her. Her own mother, who was a Scotswoman, raised her to believe that the Highlanders were nothing more than duplicitous barbarians. Was her mother mistaken?

Sensing his regard on her, she opened her eyes only to discover that his eyelids were hooded and his expression unreadable. As their gazes connected, her pulse increased as if something triggered its tempo. She was so close that she felt enthralled by the heady male scent of him. Words failed her, and she fumbled for something to say.

"Thank you for saving me," she said quickly. Her eyes dropped to his chiseled mouth, and she noticed a small crease at the bottom lip, slightly marring its male perfection. Before she dissuaded herself, she placed her hands on his shoulders, raising herself a bit before brushing a chaste kiss on his lips.

Shock appeared in his green depths.

Darra felt a blush rise to her cheeks, almost immediately regretting her rash behavior. Her bold conduct could only be attributed to her close brush with death. Pulling away, she started to apologize, but he stayed her movements. Raising a finger, he lightly traced along the curve of her bottom lip, prompting the words to suddenly die in her throat.

The expression on his striking face softened while his pupils dilated. There was a raw intensity reflected in the heavy lidded gaze, an intensity that he didn't pretend to hide. She held her breath, disbelieving that a man could be so dangerous and exciting all at once. Never had she met any man that possessed such untamed power.

With a glint in his emerald eyes, he said, "I desire a more enthusiastic thanking."

Her breath hitched in her throat, and her heart thrummed as if it threatened to burst out from her ribcage at any second. *Did he want her to kiss him again?*

As if he was aware of the frantic thoughts swirling in her mind, he fixed his gaze on her lips. If she was standing, her knees would have buckled under the magnitude of his wicked inspection. But even though they were seated, his steady regard still caused tingles to flow down her body in thrilling waves.

"Thank me again, lass," he commanded softly.

Her hand reached out and tentatively touched the side of his whiskered face, exploring the rugged contours. All the while, she was intensely aware of the solid muscular frame beneath her, and the strong corded strength that encircled her hips. He stared at her, his eyes narrowed, and his body still.

As if her fingers belonged to another woman, she watched them trail slowly along his rigid jaw. She became more emboldened when he made no protest. Darra flattened one hand on his warm cheek, and slid it around to curve at his nape. With the other palm, she slid it downward, slowly exploring his sinewy neck, down his broad shoulder until it came to rest on his bicep. The muscle flexed instinctively at her touch, and she squeezed it lightly. The strength and brawn here were born from combative training and laborious work.

She tilted her face up, and with only a small urging, she tugged his head downward to press her lips against his.

His chest expanded with a sharp inhalation, and he released a low growl. His hand reached up and cupped the back of her head as if her offering wasn't enough, and he demanded more. Much more. He increased the pressure, melding their lips together, devouring her. A wanton, mindless pleasure overwhelmed her, and she surrendered to the exquisite onslaught. *So this was how lovers kissed.*

Rory broke away for half a second, and before she could stop it, a sound of protest escaped from her lips. She looked longingly at his sensual mouth, desiring more of it.

But he took pity on her and lowered his head to possess her lips again. One large, callused hand framed the side of her face, while the other hand slid up and down her back, causing flames to spread wherever he touched.

His hot, sensual tongue ran across the seam of her lips, coaxing them apart. And when they parted under his gentle persuasion, he slipped his tongue inside her mouth. A small gasp escaped from her. Taking advantage of her surprise, his skilled tongue delved deeper into her crevice, as if starved to taste more of her honeyed essence. An inexplicable wetness formed between her legs, and a yearning so powerful rocked her.

He pivoted her smaller frame around so that she faced him. The skirt of her gown bunched up, and she attempted to tug it down.

"Nay, lass." He gently brushed her hand aside and pushed the material up higher, exposing her thighs. She felt the cool air skim against her bare skin, and she was all too aware that the only barrier between them was his great kilt and air.

He pulled her closer so that she could feel the thick ridge of his erection through the plaid.

To preserve her maidenly instincts, Darra should have jumped off Rory's lap long ago, demanding an apology. But instead, a part of her wanted to stay, wanted to learn what the fair Highlander had to offer, wanted to know why the sensations he stirred in her was so heady, so wickedly exciting.

His heated lips moved to her neck, hitting a sensitive spot, and causing her to arch her back. But the motion served to allow him better access to the tender area, and he thoroughly exploited it. She whimpered.

Rory groaned, responding to her evident pleasure. And his searing mouth moved south, finding its way to the exposed skin above the bodice of her gown. He dragged his scorching tongue along the delicate skin, licking at the area above the slopes of her breasts. The sweet torture of his erotic heat caused her nipples to pucker against the fabric of her gown. All the while a heavy ache thrummed between her thighs. And suddenly it seemed that there was too much clothing between them.

She closed her eyes and leaned into him, deeply breathing in his manly scent. The desire to taste him consumed her, and her hands went around to his steely forearms, holding onto them as if they were anchors.

Rory's large hands moved to her buttocks, tugging her abruptly forward. She was flushed against the outline of his rigid cock, and as if nothing existed between them, he circled her hips so that he rubbed her sex on his arousal.

Their kiss intensified, deepened, and ragged, fevered panting filled her ears, although she was uncertain whether the noises came from herself or from Rory.

Suddenly he tore his lips away, his breathing coming out in deep, jagged spurts.

Her eyes opened at feeling the abrupt loss of his heat, and she looked at him, confusion coiling in her head.

"I'm sorry, lass," he rasped, his chest heaving as he struggled for control. He rested his chin on the top of her head. "I didnae mean for things tae get out of hand."

Darra pushed away from him and stood up. She placed her fingers to her lips, still feeling the tingling there. But reality was flooding back to her, and she began to realize what happened, what *could have* happened.

"Do not worry over it. It will not occur again," she said.

He stood and studied her for a long moment, as if he was trying to discern her thoughts. Her fingers clenched at her skirt. What was he thinking? She felt the blood rising to her cheeks, and she braced herself for what he was going to say next. But then he surprised her by saying, "Ye must be tired. I'll carry ye back tae camp."

"Nay," she said, putting out a hand, stopping him. She couldn't risk having temptation seize her again, and rob her of her wits. His body intoxicated her, and with one touch she knew that she would soften helplessly in his arms. She might even do something that a maiden should never consider. "I will walk."

Darra began to move, to prove her resolve, but she found that her legs wobbled and she staggered slightly.

"Ye need tae conserve your strength," he said, his lips curling almost into a snarl. He bent down and easily scooped her up from the ground. "We still have a long journey ahead of us."

With her securely in his arms, he found his boots and slipped them on. Then with long, powerful strides, he made his way back toward the camp.

All that Darra could do was to circle her arms around his neck. She really had no choice, she told herself. She took a deep breath, enjoying the delicious sensation of weightlessness, of being cradled so closely, so protectively against his hard frame. And for a fleeting moment, she could even pretend that her English blood meant nothing to him, and that he truly cared for her…

Chapter 8

༄ஒஒ

Rory assessed the sleeping lass in his arms. Presently wrapped in his plaid and nestled against his chest, he felt a strange sense that this was where she belonged — with him, donning *his* plaid. Her skin was as smooth as satin, and he was tempted to brush his fingers against it, to feel its incredible softness. She had regained her color, a hint of rose staining her cheeks. When he first fished her out of the water, her face was pale and her lips blue. Her terror and fear had diminished, and her countenance now seemed peaceful, angelic.

She snuggled up to him, seeking his heat. Her innocent, trusting gesture made his heart lurch, and his grip on her tightened slightly. In such a short time, this lass managed to make him care, and he couldn't attribute it entirely to the fact that she was going to heal his father.

He shook his head, not certain where these impressions were coming from. She was from a world entirely different from his own, and would likely object if she ever knew of his thoughts. He was also well aware that she wanted to return to her home, knew that she had planned to escape from him. But after he saved her from the rushing river, she was indebted to him. He was convinced that she wouldn't run off again and would go willingly with him to the highlands.

She murmured something inaudible in her sleep. A smile suddenly formed on her pink lips, a smile suggesting that she was experiencing something pleasant in her dreams. He released a frustrated breath of air. For some reason he was attracted to Darra. She was fierce and somehow possessed an inner strength that rivaled the men he had fought with in battle. Yet she was pure feminine charm — from the soft curves of her body to her delicate, enchanting features. And her distinctive womanly scent coiled through his senses, making him dizzily aware of her. Had she been awake, he would have given in to the instinctual need to kiss her again, to recapture that peculiar sensation that she aroused in him. It was a kiss like no other, and it rocked him to his core. If they had met under different circumstances, and if she wasn't an English lass, he would have pursued her. He was long overdue to take a wife anyhow.

"I must be mad with fatigue," he muttered to himself.

Up ahead, he caught sight of her slippers near the trunk of the damaged tree. There was no point in leaving the items for the enemy to find. He shifted Darra on to one arm, and bent down to pick up the articles. Repositioning her against his shoulder, he continued on his way.

As he stepped into the campsite, he saw his brothers. They were working together to prepare oatcakes. Or rather it was Griogair who prepared the flat cakes, and Duncan, as usual, was doing the talking. While Rory didn't believe Duncan would encounter opposition in trying to leave Lancullin Castle, he was nevertheless relieved to see him relaxing by the fire.

His brothers had stacked two neat pillars of rocks on either side of the fire. They topped the structures with a stone slab, and used it as a cooking surface. At the moment, Griogair held a stick, and was about to flip a hot oatcake on to the plate when he looked up.

"Rory," he said, and then his eyes fell to the bundle in his arms. "What happened to *her*?"

Rory flipped the surplus portion of his kilt away from his shoulders, and set the lass down by the tree, which sat directly across from the small cookfire.

"She was fetching water from the river, and fell in," Rory explained.

Even as he said it, he could feel the ball of guilt churning in his gut. If he hadn't dragged her from her home, she would never have fallen into the dangerous waters.

He dusted the hem of his great kilt with the back of his hand, applying a little more force than necessary. He was determined to shake off not only the dirt but all sympathy he had for her. She was English, and it was best that he didn't forget this fact.

Glancing over at his siblings, he saw the conflicting emotions displayed on their faces. Duncan appeared suspicious while Griogair was ever watchful. None of them really wanted to be here. Hell, Rory didn't want to be here either. But they couldn't allow their father to die without making any attempt to save him.

So they required her services — at least for a short while. As soon as she healed Eanruing, Rory would compensate her for her time and trouble, and she could leave.

"We dinnae need any more water," Griogair flipped the rest of the oatcakes onto the metal plate. "I had enough in my flask tae make the meal. And I already gutted the fish I caught." He set the plate aside and went to retrieve his catch.

A soft murmur sounded, and Rory glanced over at Darra's. She stirred and stretched her arms before her eyes fluttered open. Sitting up abruptly, she looked around her, her brows pulled down in confusion.

Griogair placed the fish he had caught on the hot rock slab. The fish sizzled as it hit the scorching surface.

"Ye are at camp now," Rory told her.

She eyed the fire, but made no move to go closer to it. Instead, she pulled her knees to her chest and wrapped her arms tightly around them.

He walked over to his horse to retrieve an extra plaid from the sack. On his way back, he grabbed an oatcake and took the items over to her. Tossing her the covering, he said, "Ye can use this if ye are chilled."

She took the blanket and gratefully wrapped it around her slender shoulders.

"Take it," he crouched down to her level, and offered her the warm oatcake. "Griogair makes these for us when we travel. The fish will nae be cooked yet, but ye can eat this if ye are hungry."

"I *am* hungry," she admitted, and reached for the offering. Her hand accidentally grazed his, and she looked up at him, startled. But as soon as she made eye contact, she immediately looked to the ground. "Thank you," she said, her voice husky.

Darra held the humble oatcake, staring at it as if it was a foreign object.

"'Tis made from oats," he said, amused. "It will nae kill ye."

Duncan coughed behind him. "If ye are done, Rory," he said, "I'll need a word with ye."

Rory got up and followed him.

"Griogair told me about the gauntlet ye found," he said, unsmiling. "We need tae scope out the enemy, and glean any useful information that will assist the Queen."

"We're in enemy territory, and we dinnae ken how many we're up against," he reminded his brother. "We need tae proceed with caution."

"Tae hell with caution!" he said. "Ye ken very well that our bonny country is at stake. We're free at present, but at every turn the English try tae take our freedom away. Even now they're making their way tae steal from us. We cannae stand by, and let them seize our land." His hand clenched at the dagger that hung on his belt. "I'm leaving now tae scout the area."

"Wait," Rory said, raising his hand. "'Tis nae prudent tae scout in the growing dark. This is a strange land —"

"Da taught me tae track just as well as ye," Duncan cut in, clearly not liking the idea of waiting.

Impatience was stamped all over his younger brother's countenance. There was no way that Duncan would willingly wait, and Rory was equally aware of the importance of gathering enemy intelligence. He blew out a puff of air. "I dinnae doubt your tracking abilities, Duncan. Go and find out what we need tae ken."

Duncan started to leave when Rory placed a hand on his shoulder. "Be safe," he said.

His brother nodded. "And you as well," he said before moving away. Even in the dark, Rory knew that his sibling would find a way to get back to them. He was one of the best trackers in the highlands.

Rory watched as Duncan became swallowed up by the trees. The news that he garnered would determine their course of action. Under normal circumstances, he and Griogair would have accompanied Duncan, but they couldn't risk leaving Darra inadequately protected, or having her run off to the enemy. While it was prudent to gather military intelligence for Queen Gertrude, his main concern was to bring the healer back to Tancraig Castle.

***

With her back against the tree trunk, Darra sat across from Rory, nibbling on her fourth oatcake. She had never eaten them before, but she found them surprisingly adequate in filling the hole in her stomach.

Every once in a while she caught Rory observing her, as if he wanted to inquire after her well-being. But she was determined to ignore him and the confusing feelings that he stirred within her. Besides, she was still waiting for her chance to take flight.

Griogair had kicked off the stone slab that was blocking the fire, and the heat reaching her now made her feel warm and drowsy. Her grip on the plaid relaxed, and the material slipped from her shoulders. Exhaustion washed over her, and she leaned her head against the tree bark.

Duncan had just returned from his excursion, and judging by the serious tone of their voices, the brothers would likely converse long into the night.

Darra closed her eyes, listening to their Scottish burrs. The soft lilt of their voices had a strange musical quality to it, a quality that was lulling her to sleep.

She was about to drift off when something Duncan said jolted her awake. Were they speaking about the English cavalry? Her heart began to speed up, and she fought to keep the smile from spreading across her face. Her opportunity was about to materialize, and her captors would divulge all that she needed to know.

Making a show of yawning and stretching, she lowered herself onto the ground, making sure that she faced the trio.

"Where exactly are they located?" Griogair asked.

"Half a mile down river. 'Twas nae difficult tae see where they camped as they had a dozen cookfires scattered near each other."

"A dozen, ye say," Rory said thoughtfully.

"Aye, there were at least fifteen men sitting around one fire pit," Duncan said, his tone flat. *"The other fire pits had the same number of men, I ken."* He fiddled with a stick in his hand and tapped it rhythmically on the ground. *"They had a cart full of heavy armory that they abandoned outside one of the sites."*

While the brothers fell silent, the wood in the fire hissed gently as the heat evaporated the water that was trapped inside.

In the meantime, her heart thumped heavily in her chest with the knowledge and elation that freedom was only half a mile away. If she made her way to the English camps, she would find the sanctuary that she needed. After that, the king's men would escort her safely home.

She continued to watch the three brothers through the narrow slits of her eyes, although she no longer paid attention to what they were saying. All she required now was for them to fall asleep, and then she would make her escape.

An eternity seemed to pass before the men banked the fire and sought their beds. Duncan and

Griogair slept adjacent to the small campfire. Using a portion of their great kilts as blankets, they pulled the material to cover their heads. Meanwhile Rory found his place a foot away from her.

Darra let out a slow breath, her excitement ready to burst. Soon enough the crisp air was filled with the sounds of the night — leaves rustling in the tree canopies, the occasional cricket chirping, the ever flowing river in the distance, *and* snoring.

She waited several more minutes, clutching her hand to her chest. Her heart was racing, and she feared that the frantic beating would disturb the slumbering men. Rolling her head to the side, she observed her captors. While part of their kilts covered their heads, the faces of Rory and Griogair were bared. Duncan meanwhile had his entire head concealed in his plaid. None of them moved, and the snores and deep even breathing continued unabated.

Slowly, she lifted herself onto her knees. Then careful not to make a sound, she crawled away from her captors. Just when she made it to the outer edge of the campsite, she got up to run. Unfortunately her foot slipped on the wet earth, and she fell forward.

For a split second, she lay stunned, but then seized by fear and panic that the Highlanders might catch her, she scrambled up from the ground and bolted. She jumped over the logs that were in her way and crashed through the underbrush.

She quickly found the river's edge, and paused only long enough to determine the downward flow of the river. Then she tore through the uneven ground, her mind focusing on one thing — getting to her saviors.

After running for a long while, she slowed down to catch her breath. The commotions of the forest seemed amplified. And the hooting owl overhead mocked her for foolishly wandering alone in the darkness. Everyone knew that the woods was a frightening place to roam. And at night, it was also an eerie and dangerous place. All the stories that she heard as a child came to the forefront, causing gooseflesh to form on her arms. There were many creatures that hid in the shadows, and whether they were mortal or not was uncertain. While some of them were harmless, some others might be malevolent. She prayed that this wasn't the time that she encountered the evil and terrifying ones.

Darra started to move again when she saw a stick poking out from the thicket. That was it! She needed a weapon to defend herself against anything harmful.

As she walked toward the stick, a thorny branch snagged her gown. She bent down to free herself when a rustling in the bushes nearby made her jump. Darra scrambled to reach for the stick when a branch lashed across her face. Letting out a startled cry, she fell backward.

The rustling became louder.

With a scream trapped in the back of her throat, she lay paralyzed on the ground, staring at the area where the noise originated. A small break in the tree tops allowed enough light to illuminate the shrubbery. Any moment now, the creature would emerge and devour her.

And it did emerge, except it was small, and the familiar black and white headed critter scurried past her.

"A badger!" she said, disbelief and relief flooding into her body all at once.

Taking a staggering breath, she surveyed her surroundings. How far was she exactly? Nothing was recognizable, and as far as she could tell, she might be wandering around in circles.

Still, there was no way she could go back to her brawny captors. She saw an opening between two trees and started toward them. She had only taken a couple of steps when a flash of light caught the corner of her eye. Darra twisted around, and before she could stop it, a gasp escaped from her lips. It was a knight making water at the tree!

"Who's there?" he called out, his voice slurred. He pulled up his hose. Lifting his lamp in the air with unsteady hands, he swayed slightly as he peered into the darkness. His other hand reached for the sword at his belt.

He was a large, rough-looking knight who was obviously inebriated. But she sensed something else about him, something that was decidedly sinister. He didn't appear anything like the savior that she had in mind. In fact, she suspected that he would rather rape and kill her before he took her to his commander.

She ducked behind the nearest tree, and crouched down. Trying to make herself as small as possible, she prayed that the darkness hid her.

Darra could hear his footsteps coming closer. And then to her relief, the steps moved past her.

She let out a small sigh and crawled to find a better hiding place among the shrubbery. She was closing in on the bushes when she felt something jerk hard at her hair.

Searing pain ripped through her head, and she shrieked.

"A woman," the knight spat. There was disgust in his voice, but then he bent down to take a closer look at her face. Suddenly, as if the drunken haze cleared, his eyes widened in surprise before it narrowed into a disturbing leer.

"Have mercy, sire! I am your ally!" she cried desperately.

He burst out into a guffaw that was punctuated by noisy snorts.

"Ally?" he said, lifting the back of his hand up to wipe at the spittle. "A *woman* ally? I've never heard such a jest."

"I wish you to take me to your commander," she said, trying to interject authority into her voice, although it trembled as she spoke.

The knight threw back his head, and started laughing again as if it was the funniest thing he had ever heard.

But then there was a powerful *thunk*, and the laughter died as fast as it had started.

The grip on her hair loosened. The drunken knight fell to the ground with a thud, and the lamp crashed to the forest floor. But just before the light from the lamp sputtered out, she caught a glimpse of furious green eyes.

Chapter 9

৶৽

Rory found it was easy to track Darra down. She made enough noise to alert the entire forest of her presence. His long strides had almost caught up with her when she suddenly ran to a tree and squatted. He frowned and instinctively melted into the shadows.

Darra huddled at the base of the tree like a rabbit who was cowering from a fox. She was in danger, he realized. His heart thudded dully in his chest, and a chill crept over his flesh. Somehow he sensed that it wasn't an animal that frightened her. He cursed softly under his breath. She was thoughtless to run away from his protection. Didn't she know how hazardous it was to be alone in the woods and at night?

Still, even in her folly, he couldn't allow anything to harm her. No matter how reckless she was, he was responsible for keeping her safe.

He edged to the opposite end where a thick band of shrubbery grew, and peeked over. And sure enough, there was a man advancing slowly toward Darra's hiding place. There was nowhere for her to run, and any movement she made would give her away. Even

Rory couldn't go to her since his presence would endanger them both.

The knight walked past her, and Rory thought she would stay put, except she went on her knees and started to crawl away from her hiding spot.

Stop! he wanted to shout, but it was too late. The guard, who was about to leave, swung around, lifting his lamp high while his free hand reached for his sword. When he discovered the fetching lass, he appeared especially gleeful.

Rory sighed. There was only one thing left for him to do. Seeing a large rock nearby, he bent down and picked it up. Then jumping out from his cover, he slammed the rock on the man's crown, taking him by surprise. While the knight was still stunned, Rory wrapped his arm around the other man's neck, squeezing the air out of it. An awful choking sound emerged from the knight's lips while he clawed frantically at Rory's arm. But the guard was too weakened by drink, and was unable to fight him. A split second later, his movements ceased, and he slumped forward.

Rory dropped the knight, his body hitting the ground with a thump.

"I wouldnae want tae ally myself with that drunken bastard," he said.

"You saved me," she said, her voice shaky.

"I dinnae ken why," he said, offering her his hand. She took it, and he pulled her up from the ground. "Ye seem tae have a knack for getting into trouble."

A mirthless laugh escaped from her. Her regard dropped to where the intoxicated knight had collapsed. Swallowing, she turned and gave Rory a tight smile. "Thank you once again for saving me."

He grunted in answer. Now that she was safe, relief and anger twisted inside his gut. Where did these emotions come from? He shouldn't be having any feelings toward this lass. She was the means to help his father and nothing more. When he bedded down for the night, he had no intentions of traipsing through the dark forest in search for a runaway lass. And it certainly didn't help matters that the woman standing in front of him was so damn tempting.

"This way." He grabbed her wrist and pulled her behind him. "Ye are still in danger."

"Why did ye run away from the safety of our camp?" he demanded.

Darra opened her mouth and closed it again. She couldn't very well tell him that she wanted to escape him and his brothers, and that she had no intentions of leaving England.

"Do you know where we are?" she asked, changing the topic.

"Nay, but I do ken that we're far from my brothers. For such a wee lass, ye cover quite a bit of ground." He scanned the trees. "We need tae go deeper into the woods sae that we willnae stumble upon any English camps."

"But what of the knight?"

"He willnae be following us," he said, shaking his head. "Your knight was too drunk tae ken what happened tae him."

Darra nodded and sighed with relief. She shuddered to think what would have happened if Rory hadn't come along.

Setting a rapid pace, Rory dragged her along. But the excitement of the night was catching up with her, and she stumbled. His sinewy arm snaked around her waist, and caught her before she fell headlong into the tangle of roots.

"Are ye all right, lass?" he asked, his brows knitted with concern.

"Aye," she said.

Her side was flushed against his, and a shot of electricity flowed through her. The sudden shock of it almost made her wrench from his embrace.

He glanced briefly down at her, a small frown on his ruggedly handsome countenance. She drew in a deep breath through her nose, unwittingly taking in his musky and unmistakable male scent. Everything about him was appealing — except for the fact that he was a Scotsman and a heathen, she reminded herself sternly. But even so, she was dangerously attracted to him.

She twisted her lips to the side. What was it about this powerful man that was so alluring? And why did she want to kiss him again and reawaken the mystifying and intoxicating sensations that he roused in her?

Rory continued to watch her, a knowing expression on his visage. His eyes lowered briefly to her lips. When he looked up again, his gaze fixed onto hers. The heat radiating from him was palpable, and it scared and excited her all at once. No man had ever made her feel this way. But this was ridiculous! Of all things, she shouldn't be pondering these lustful thoughts. Instead, she should be focusing on placing one foot in front of the other, and plotting another way to get home.

They traveled for another hour, and by this time, she was no longer able to think.

"I need to rest," she said, panting. "It feels as though we have been walking for hours. Are we lost?"

When he didn't respond, she eyed him through her peripheral vision. He stopped to take measure of the trees that surrounded them. For a fleeting moment, she witnessed uncertainly in his countenance.

"We *are* lost," she gasped as the truth hit her.

"We will stay here until daybreak," he said, neglecting to acknowledge her conclusions.

He kicked away at some rocks and twigs on the ground. Then walking over to a nearby tree, he sat down and leaned his head on the trunk. "Sleep," he said, gesturing to the space in front of him. "I'll keep watch."

Darra had no energy to argue with him, and the forest floor seemed inviting enough. She sank gratefully onto the soft ground. Closing her eyes, she willed herself to fall asleep.

But sleep eluded her. She had worked up sweat from traipsing through the woods. Now that she was no longer moving, the perspiration had cooled on her skin, making her feel cold and uncomfortable. Flipping over onto her side, she pulled her arms closer to her chest and curled into a tight ball to preserve her own heat. All the while she wished that she had a woolen blanket to cut out the autumn chill.

The wind picked up, and she heard the loud swishing and rustling of the leaves above. Under normal circumstances, the whispering trees might have soothed her nerves, but now they seemed menacing and otherworldly. She took a deep breath. There is nothing to fear, she told herself.

Was Rory still by the tree? She twisted around to look at where he sat. Relieved, she saw that he hadn't moved from his spot. But that relief was short-lived. Just when she was about to shut her eyes again, the howl of a lone wolf rose above the sweeping leaves.

Her eyes popped open.

She pushed herself into a seated position. There would be no sleep tonight. She was well aware that if she slept, she was easy fodder for any wild animal that stumbled upon her. In addition, there were the malicious forest spirits which she needed to guard against. Darra had never met the evil creatures, but she realized that she was trespassing on their domain. She swallowed, and felt a sudden urge to be closer to Rory.

"What is the matter?" he asked, his deep voice carrying over to her.

"I heard a wolf," she said, tightening her arms around her chest.

"We are in a forest," he shrugged. "There are bound to be wolves roaming about."

As if to punctuate the truth of his words, the wolf howled again in the distance, the sound echoing eerily in the night. She swung her head in the direction of the noise. Wolves traveled in packs. What if they decided to come here and attack them?

He stood up and sighed. "Come with me, lass. Ye are shivering."

As much as she wanted to refuse him, his offer was like a gift. His hand closed around her icy fingers, and she allowed him to lead her to the tree. Settling back down, he pulled her down to sit on his lap.

He took the plaid that was draped over his shoulders, and wrapped it over both of them. His warmth immediately enveloped her.

Suddenly the tiredness and fear that gripped her earlier were gone. Somehow she sensed that he would keep her safe from any wild beast or evil spirit, although now she had a new worry. Rory's distinct masculine scent encased her, and with her curves pressed intimately against his hard planes, her flesh tingled with heightened awareness.

She started to shift, trying to get away from the strange sensation.

"Would ye cease your squirming," Rory said, his voice tight.

Darra moved again until she was able to look at him. His features were in shadow, but she could still feel the weight of his stare.

"Tell me, what is the real reason why you have come to England," she said, wanting to distract herself with conversation rather than think about their close proximity.

He hesitated as if pondering whether or not he would answer her question. And just when she thought that he wouldn't respond, he said, "Ye are my last resort."

"Me?" she asked, surprised.

"Aye," he nodded. "Ye, your mother — whoever has the ability tae heal my da. I dinnae want death tae take him away sae soon." He paused, his voice sounding far away. "When I was a lad, I was fooling with my brothers. We climbed a tree, swinging and jumping on the branches. In a moment of carelessness, I slipped and fell. I broke all the bones in my legs." A wry smile appeared on his lips. "Everyone gave up on me, branding me a cripple. But 'twas my da who believed that I would be whole again. He patiently helped me tae heal, and tae walk again. And so now 'tis he who has fallen ill. Everyone has given up on him, but nae me. I believe that he will be healed of whatever ails him."

"You came here out of love for your father," she said softly.

"Aye," he said, clearing his throat as if he realized that he had revealed too much. "Time is running out, and we need tae get back tae the highlands. Will ye come with me, and help my da?"

She could hear the appeal in his voice. He would no longer force her, but would ask for her permission. Even though she tried to fight it, sympathy swirled in her heart. Her own father had died, and there wasn't any way to save him. But with Rory's father, she could perhaps make a difference.

"All right" she said, "I will go with you."

He dropped his head and pressed his lips briefly to hers.

Her eyes widened. "Why did you do that?" she asked.

"Tae thank ye of course," he grinned. Then he grew silent. "Why do ye have tae be English?" he asked, his tone turning serious.

"I am a person, not a country," she said.

"Aye, 'tis the truth of it." Rory let out a long sigh. He reached up and caressed her cheek with a finger and trailed it down to trace over her lips. "Ye sorely tempt me, ye ken. Having tasted these sweet lips once before, I find that I want more."

His soft words caused a wave of heat to roll down to her core. "Until you, no one has ever kissed me like that," she admitted.

He tightened his hold on her, drawing her closer. "I'm glad," he said, his breath hot against her lips. And before she could say anything further, his mouth touched hers, the gesture tender, tentative, as if allowing her to break away if she wanted. But she wished to continue. Her fingers drifted along his muscular forearms, up to his broad shoulders until they finally threaded through his coppery hair.

He lifted her from his lap and positioned her so that her legs were spread on either side of him.

An innate urge to seek his heat caused her to move closer.

He groaned.

"Ye will drive me insane, lass," he said, breathing harshly. He placed his hands on her hips, and started to gently push her away.

"Please," she said.

Rory paused at hearing her plea.

She reached up with both hands and cupped his whiskered cheeks. A feeling of recklessness came over her. She took a deep breath and plunged onward. "I have never experienced passion like this before. I want...more..."

"Ye dinnae ken what ye are wanting, lass," he said slowly.

"But I do know," she said, licking her lips. His heated gaze fastened onto the quick movement.

Sir Dudley, the lord in the neighboring castle, wanted to marry her. He had wanted to marry her for a long time now. But the thought of kissing the old knight repelled her as much as kissing a toad. And the notion of sleeping in his bed made her shudder. However with Rory, it was different. He made her feel alive, and she desired everything that he had to offer. Without a doubt she knew that he offered a wild love — a love that Sir Dudley could never deliver.

"In my entire existence I have been a careful, dutiful daughter," she explained. He cocked his head, listening to her speak. "A knight favors my hand in marriage, and I will likely do my part and marry him. But I want to experience the fervor, the kind of ardor the bards sing about. I want to taste it, savor it just this once before I must fulfill my duty, and before I grow old and gray." She let out a deep breath. "Surely there is no harm in this, is there?"

He stood, pulling her up with him. Looking down at her, a fierce, unreadable expression flitted across his face.

"Are ye certain about this?" he demanded. His fists were resting on his lean hips — a picture of masculine strength and beauty.

"Aye," she nodded, her heart beginning to thud with excitement and anticipation.

"Very well," he said, loosening the notch on the belt that held his great kilt together. Taking the material, Rory folded it in half before laying it on the ground.

He straightened, and all that he had on was a *leine*. The shirt stretched tightly across his massive shoulders and dropped to his mid-thigh. He moved where there was a break in the tree canopy. Then as if he was fully aware that she watched, he lifted his muscular arms, tugged the linen shirt off, and dropped it to the ground.

Her breath caught as she took in his naked form. The soft light reflected off his tawny skin, casting shadows on his torso, and defining the taut ridges along his abdomen. Her curious eyes followed the sculpted ridges of his physique, and widened when she caught sight of his erection. Her cheeks flushed and she averted her face.

"Nay lass, look at me."

She blinked, and did as he commanded. He was big. She had no idea a man could be that large.

He walked over, and brought her to the break in the trees.

"Now 'tis my turn tae look at ye," he said, chuckling.

His hands went down and with expert fingers, he unlaced her gown, revealing her chemise. When she left the castle, Fyfa had dressed her quickly and didn't bother to put on her corset and outer gown. But now as Darra stood in her undergarment, she felt exposed and vulnerable.

His palms smoothed down the length of her, pausing to cup her breasts before bunching the material in his fists, and dragging the thin chemise over her head. He dropped the shift to the ground.

Reaching for her hand, he held it in the air as he took in a deep, appreciative breath. "My god, ye are a bonny lass," he murmured. His heated stare took away the chill of the night. Hunger reflected in his eyes as they swept over her naked body, lingering on her chest. Her nipples hardened in response to his intense scrutiny, and her breasts became heavy and swollen with need. A blush rose to her cheeks, and she attempted to cover herself with her hands.

"Nay," Rory said, gently tugging her hands away. "I want tae see ye — all of ye."

He drew her toward him, smoothing his large hands over her shoulders. And although his hands only brushed her skin, they felt as hot as burning coals. As their naked bodies touched, she felt molten fire cascading down her entire length and settling at the juncture between her legs. And suddenly she wanted, needed more. At this moment.

Then obeying an innate compulsion, she leaned in and rubbed her sensitive breasts against his hard chest. Her aching nubs raked across the firm flesh of his torso. She wasn't an innocent maiden; she already knew what was going to happen next. With many years of apprenticeship, and with her mother patiently answering all of her questions, Darra understood about the relations between men and women. And though she was aware of the mechanics of lovemaking, and in producing offspring, it never occurred to her that there was more involved. Now with her curiosity piqued, her body craved that carnal knowledge. And Rory, it seemed, was eager to instruct her.

He wrapped one arm around the upper portion of her back and the other arm under her buttocks, drawing her to him. Almost immediately, she felt the insistent press of his arousal against her stomach.

"Darra," he groaned. Dipping his head, he captured her lips in a lingering, exquisite kiss. All the while, his hands ran restlessly up and down her back, causing a trail of flames to ignite wherever he touched.

Her eyes closed as the roar of rushing blood filled her ears. She had a vague sense of weightlessness, as if her entire body was being lifted to the clouds.

He ran the tip of his tongue along her lips, urging them to part. And when they did, he slipped his tongue inside, dipping into, and drinking from her as if he discovered sweet ambrosia there.

His breathing became harsh, and he tightened his grip, deepening the kiss. Rory's wicked tongue tangled with hers, stroking it, sucking it, and acting out the ancient dance between man and woman. She felt a slippery wetness between her thighs, and she wondered about the sensation.

Then almost as if he heard her thoughts, his hand skimmed down her sensitive skin. When he reached the curls that covered her sex, he dipped one finger inside her.

"Ye are wet for me," he said, groaning.

Bending, he lifted her in his arms, and took her to the plaid that he had set on the ground. He gently placed her at the center of the fabric, and then without breaking contact with her, he settled between her legs. She could feel his velvety hardness nudging against her thighs. Instinctively, she opened her legs wider to accommodate him.

Rory's hand reached back down to her mound. His finger found her clitoris, teasing, circling it until she was moaning in tortured ecstasy.

He bent his head and began to kiss the side of her neck, moving to the tender spot slightly behind her ear. When he licked her there, her back arched in response. Slowly he moved over her body, showering hot attention over one breast. She sucked in a sharp breath and gripped his head.

When his searing mouth left the swollen breast, the cool air swept over it, leaving her bereft. But before she could object, his scorching lips found the other breast, paying it equal homage. Her fingers laced through his red hair, grabbing it as he flattened his tongue across her flesh and scraped it across the hardened nub. She shuddered under the blissful onslaught.

Rory looked up and caught her watching him. A mischievous smile lit his eyes and pointing his tongue, he flicked it on her distended nipple. Her chest abruptly thrust upward in shock. He chuckled and before she could recover, he bent down again. Hollowing his cheeks, he sucked hard on the puckered tit.

She writhed under his amorous attack. Just when she thought she couldn't take it any longer, he left her breast and trailed a wet path down her torso. Closing her eyes, she surrendered herself to his wicked tongue as it continued to drag across her bared flesh.

But then he stopped.

She opened her eyes and saw that he shifted downward, and was kneeling between her legs.

"I want to taste more of ye," he said.

Her eyebrows furrowed slightly. "I do not underst —" The last of her words were cancelled out by a gasp. And any further attempts to discern what he meant faded into the nether recess of her mind. His strong fingers dug into her hips, lifting her high. Leaning forward, he gave her a lush open-mouthed kiss on her most intimate place.

She felt a sudden gush release within her, and he began to devour her as if he was a starving man. His tongue moved faster, frantically swiping, stoking at a region that had never known a man's touch. She lifted her hips higher, crying as she yielded to him. A new pressure built up inside her, growing, expanding until it exploded in a colorful wave of euphoria and bliss.

When he raised his head again, his eyes were gleaming. "I thought that ye would enjoy that," he said.

She shook her head, unable to speak. Was this something that she would experience if she married Sir Dudley? Somehow she doubted it.

He moved up, allowing his torso to skim across her flesh. "Just sae ye ken," he said. "We are far from finished."

He braced his elbows on either side of her while his hard, hot shaft settled on her sex. Then pressing forward slightly, he allowed her to feel the swollen tip of his cock.

Sweat beaded on his forehead as he fought for control. He pushed his hips a little further. "I'm only sorry that this part will hurt ye."

And then in one smooth motion, he pushed past her maidenly barrier, embedding his entire rod into her.

A sharp gasp escaped from her lips. Her body lurched upward, and her nails dug into his shoulders. He paused, his face twisted in torment and restraint. Little by little, the pain receded, and she wondered at the strange and wonderful fullness that was now in her.

Rory buried his head in her hair briefly before he raised himself onto his hands. Then he looked down at her, and gritted his teeth as if it took momentous effort to keep himself still.

"Are ye all right, lass?" he grounded out.

"Aye," she said. But she didn't have a chance to say anything further. The breath hitched in her chest as he began to move — slow at first and then faster. A few seconds more, and she felt the intense, blistering heat swelling between them, could hear the wet, slick sounds as their bodies unified and parted. And as he drove her higher, her breath burst out in jagged pants. Her fingers gripped his shoulders as she met his thrust with her own. Her body understood instinctively what it was searching for. As they found their rhythm, a torrid heat amplified within her, the pressure climbing, climbing until finally it erupted into an explosion of energy.

Reaching up, she blindly pulled his lips to hers, wanting him to share in her ecstasy. She found his tongue, drawing it into her mouth, sucking at it. His muscular frame jerked, tensed. Then he began to rock his hips against her as a primal groan rumbled through his powerful chest and he released his seed into her.

Suddenly he fell on to his corded forearms, his weight braced there so that she wouldn't be crushed.

"That was incredible," he said in awe.

"Aye, it *was* incredible," was all that she managed to say. And it was something that she would never experience again.

Chapter 10

❧❧

Darra felt a delicious warmth against her cheek, and she wondered whether she was dreaming. Coming slowly into consciousness, she heard the birds twittering overhead. Her fingertips skimmed over smooth skin and hard muscle. Right beneath her ear, she heard a solid, rhythmic heart beating...

Hard muscle? Heart beating?

The questions crashed through her mind like a battering ram at the gates. She jerked back her hand, and became even more alarmed to find herself cradled against Rory's taut, masculine torso. Her first impulse was to leap off his lap, but then she glanced down and discovered that she was nude. Images from last night flooded her mind. So it wasn't a dream after all; she really had made love with Rory.

But the pleasant memory soon changed into something more worrisome. Now that it was morning, she was confronted with the cold, hard truth that she was no longer a virgin. She blinked at this startling fact. Her innocence was lost the moment she decided to kiss Rory. But now that she experienced how raw, primal love felt, she desired more — even though this was supposed to be a one-time occurrence. She released a shuddering sigh.

"Ye are awake," Rory's deep voice penetrated her thoughts.

"Oh," she tipped her head back. His expression was impassive, as if he wasn't fazed that a naked woman slept in his arms. "I thought you were still asleep."

"Nay, all parts of me are definitely awake," he said, a sudden mischievous gleam reflecting in his eyes.

A part of him was definitely poking at her hip. She felt fire rush to her face just as a sharp tingle coursed through her, and thrummed between her legs. She came off his lap, found her chemise and quickly put it on.

Spinning around to face him, she declared, "Last night was a mistake." But the real mistake was to look at him. In the gray light, she was able to see him in all his glory. He remained sitting, a mildly amused expression on his visage. As she wondered at his amusement, a small movement from his hand caught her attention, drawing her scrutiny downward.

Her breath caught in her windpipe.

With one hand, he gripped his magnificent cock, stroking its thick length while he watched her with hooded eyes.

"'Twas a mistake," she said again, tearing her gaze away from his obvious male pleasure, and ignoring the intense flames that blazed through her system. She released a shaky breath. These unwelcome feelings made her feel unsettled and confused. As soon as she finished healing Eanruing MacGregon, she would go back to England, and forget about all the curious sensations that Rory roused in her. It was foolish to develop any attachment to this man. She tasted passion once, and it should be enough, shouldn't it?

Rory stood and stretched, his muscles rippling as he moved. He made a striking figure clothed in his great kilt, but standing naked, he was spectacular, breathtaking. He appeared unconscious or unconcerned about his male beauty, and the fact that he bore a raging cockstand.

"If ye are keen," he grinned. "I'm willing to make another mistake."

At his words, the heat in her cheeks burned even more. She found her kirtle and quickly dressed. When she turned back to him, she was relieved that he had donned his *leine*. Still, she didn't feel safe staring at his lithe and powerful form, since underneath that shirt, she knew that he was stark naked.

"We should leave," she said awkwardly.

He chuckled as if he could read her thoughts. Taking the plaid that was draped over his arm, he arranged it on the ground.

She averted her face, but she still saw him in her peripheral vision. With practiced hands, he pleated the material before laying it on the ground and belted it around his narrow hips. As he stood up, he slung the excess fabric over one broad shoulder and secured it into place with a wide brooch.

"Thank you for saving me from that knight," she said, relieved that he was now fully dressed.

"Ye wouldnae have required saving if ye had stayed asleep," he said, attaching his sporran onto his belt and then looping his sword belt across his chest. "Next time ye may nae be as fortunate."

A tremor rolled over her. She knew that he spoke the truth. Before this incident, she was ready and willing to escape from him and his brothers. However she began to recognize that it was less perilous to remain with the Highlanders. If she had gotten to the cavalry, and the army turned out to be as dishonorable and uncaring as the drunken knight, then her fate would have been wretched indeed.

"We should get to your father as soon as possible," she said.

He quirked an eyebrow at her. "So ye will hold true tae your promise, and willnae longer run off again?"

"Aye," she said. "I will heal your father, and once I am finished, you can escort me home."

"I can agree tae that," he said. "Let's go then. The English cavalry will be awake and active soon. I would loathe tae run into them, ye ken."

She nodded and surveyed the dense forest that encompassed her.

"How will we find the others?" she asked.

"We go this way," Rory said.

"But how do you know which route to take?" she asked. "I thought we were lost last night."

He stopped and crouched down to pick up a broken twig. "Ye made more noise than the *Shellycoat* and his rattling shells. And ye left an easy trail tae follow." He tossed the stick into the bushes. "We'll just need tae find your tracks again, and find our way back tae camp." Her eyes widened as if he had just revealed the ancient secrets of the forest. He shrugged. "'Tis much easier tae see your tracks in the morning light." He swept the area where they slept with his foot, tossing up the dirt and erasing all evidence of their stay. "Now nay one will ken that we were here. This way, lass."

Rory stepped forward, not bothering to look behind him, since he fully expected her to follow.

The dawning light broke through the trees, and the forest was alive with the clamor of foraging animals.

"How much further do we have to go?" she asked, panting while trying to keep up with him.

He didn't answer her. Obviously she didn't realize how much ground that she covered when she raced away from their campsite. Danger lurked here, and they needed to get back to the site before they were discovered.

They traveled for at least an hour before he slowed his pace. He sensed that they were close to the site, and was also aware of Darra's tiredness.

Soon enough the campsite came into view. At first, he felt relief at seeing the familiar tree that marked their spot, but in the next moment he was overcome with a niggling sense that something was wrong.

Searching behind him, he observed that the area that they emerged from was still encased in darkness. Under normal circumstances, the noisy chatter of birds would be rampant at this time. But the forest was strangely silent.

A breeze caught at his hair as he surveyed the empty space. If he didn't know any better, he would never have believed that this area was used as a refuge. In fact the only sign of human habitation was the stone cooking surface that lay on the ground; there was no trace of the men or their horses. A sudden anger surged to his chest, although it wasn't directed at anyone but himself. Had he inadvertently brought the enemy to his unsuspecting brothers? And if the bastards took them, were they now being beaten and tortured?

Darra, not realizing that he had stopped, bumped into his back.

"What is the matter?" she asked, grabbing onto his arm as she found her balance.

"They're gone," he said, through clenched teeth. He reached behind him and withdrew his claymore.

"Who —?" she started to ask, and stopped when she saw the sword in his hands. Her jaw dropped open. "Do you think the royal cavalry has come upon them?" she whispered. Her face had gone pale, as if she believed that she was to blame for his brothers' disappearance.

"I dinnae ken," he said, unable to keep the vexation from his voice. "If the knights found my brothers, they'll nae give them mercy. And if they're nae killed on the spot, they'll be taken tae the English court tae be hanged as traitors." His tone turned bitter. "Anyone who opposes your King Harold is a traitor, ye ken."

Rory gave the area another sweeping glance, his shoulders rigid with tension. His father had to wait. His priority now was to find his brothers, and free them from the enemies.

Bending down to the forest floor, he searched for clues. He would have to scour the site thoroughly in order to determine which direction to take. Fortunately he could trust Griogair to leave some sort of trail for him to follow.

"Rory," Darra said nervously. "I think I heard something."

He shook his head, not wanting the distraction. He had to concentrate. But then his head shot up when he heard a soft, whispery movement in the bushes. Tilting his head, he tried to listen for the sound again. And there it was. But this time the noise was followed immediately by the unmistakable nicker of a horse.

Reaching over, he pulled Darra behind him, shielding her from whoever was approaching.

Dropping into a fighting stance, he held his claymore in front of him, his gaze fixed intently at the spot where he heard the noise.

Unexpectedly Duncan's familiar form atop a horse emerged from the thicket. A second later, Griogair rode in with Rory's horse in tow.

Rory hissed and lowered his sword.

"Where the hell were ye two?" he growled.

Duncan urged his horse forward, eying the sword. "A better question would be: where the hell were ye? We woke up, and the two of ye were gone. I thought perhaps the English had taken ye."

"Aye," Griogair said, joining in. "That was the thought that went through my mind as well. We went tae higher ground tae see if we could spot ye. And when we didnae see ye, we circled back here."

"We're safe for now," Rory said, sliding his claymore back into its sheath. He lifted Darra onto his horse's back before mounting behind her. "Let's be gone from this place."

Chapter 11

"We're home," Rory said in relief. They had managed to cross the border unscathed.

Off in the distance, he could see the outlines of his beloved mountains. He didn't know how it was possible, but once they traversed into his bonny country, he felt an energy shift. The world seemed quieter, more arresting. He exhaled deeply, releasing the tension that plagued him from the moment he stepped foot on to English territory.

Even though they were passing through the moorlands, he could detect the clean, fresh scent of mountain air, and the pungent fragrance of pine needles from a nearby forest. The autumn had transformed most of the wild grass into brown, red and gold threads. Meanwhile patches of purple heather grew among the vegetation, lending a breathtaking vividness to the craggy landscape.

Darra sat in front of him. Ever since Rory rescued her from the English cavalry, she had been quiet. No doubt she realized that she was far safer with him than with her countrymen. She sat with her back as straight as a rod, as if she was afraid to touch him. The lass seemed all together different from the one who surrendered to him mere hours before.

Suddenly she turned and spoke over her shoulder. "How much further do we need to go until we get to your home?"

The sun was overhead, and they had already been riding for hours. But he didn't dare stop even though he noted the dark circles under her eyes.

"Likely about four more hours of riding," he said. "However we'll go at a slower rate, and will continue tae proceed with caution."

"But why?" she asked, her blue eyes bright with curiosity.

"'Tis because we are nae yet out of danger," Duncan said, exasperation in his voice. "We're moving into the Lochclay territory. If we're not careful, those bastards will swoop down like birds of prey and come after us."

"Lochclay?" she repeated, her brows furrowing. "Why those would be my mother's kin…"

Rory nodded. "The Lochclays have no love for us."

"And we have no love for them," Griogair added, his tone a matter of fact.

She regarded Griogair, her expression unreadable. And then she surveyed all around her as if to search for the hostile clans that they spoke about. "I thought 'twas only the English that you opposed," she said finally.

"Nay," Rory said. "We oppose the English, but we also have enemies within our own borders. As we have a common cause tae drive out the English, we've formed a precarious truce with the other clans."

"Clan Lochclay has fought along side us in the last war," Griogair said. "But I wouldnae trust them."

"I wouldnae either," Duncan nodded. "But as the English are set tae attack again, the queen will reunite the clans." Stopping, he raised his hand to shield his eyes. "Look, I see the village up ahead." He flashed a grin at Griogair. "I'll race ye."

***

The brothers thundered ahead while Rory and Darra followed at a slower pace. They rode through a small village where stone houses clustered together. Off in the distance, Darra saw an enormous castle.

A man and his son stopped in their task and waved to Rory. But when they noticed her, their scrutiny dropped abruptly to her gown and then flew back to her face. From the frown on their faces, it was obvious that they saw her as an unwanted foreigner. Though she pretended that she couldn't sense their hostilities, she still felt the sting in her heart. She focused her attention on the looming castle, wishing that circumstances actually favored her, and that she was presently making her way out of Scotland. But of course, it was only a wish, and she was indebted to Rory.

"Your clansmen do not like me," she said, drawing in a shaky breath.

"'Tis because ye are a *sassenach*," Rory said dismissively. "But they'll get used tae ye soon enough."

When they arrived at Tancraig Castle, Darra noted that two women and two youths waited for them. Their expressions were joyous when they saw Rory riding toward them. But like the townspeople, their demeanor became wary and unfriendly once they noticed Darra sitting in front of their brother. The dark-haired lass, who appeared to be the eldest, stepped forward first while her younger siblings followed suit.

Rory dismounted from the horse. As he turned to help Darra down from the horse, he caught the uncertainty in her eyes. She sent him a tremulous smile, and immediately the sense of guilt reignited in his chest. But he pushed aside his remorse, and focused on the business at hand. He reached over and pulled the sack that hung from his horse. Digging in, he pulled out her medicine basket and handed it to her.

"I'll have one of my brothers take ye tae see Eanruing," he said.

She clutched the basket to her stomach as if it was a shield. The sun reflected off her flaxen hair, and he saw her blink, likely wishing that she was anywhere but here. He recognized the cold reception that his clan members gave to Darra, and he perceived that they didn't want a *sassenach* in their midst. And neither did his siblings, even though they knew better. Rory blew out a rush of air and ran his fingers through his hair in frustration. He couldn't very well reprimand his kin for the emotions they held in their hearts. After all, they had every right to hate the English. Those bastards had killed and maimed too many people they loved. Nay, the English deserved every last drop of hatred that they could muster. He was just unconvinced that this lass was the one who deserved the full brunt of their animosity.

Cailean approached the horses, and started to take them to the stables.

"Wait a minute, Cailean," he said. His younger brother paused. "I want Lady Darra to meet everyone."

He placed his hand at the curve of her back. "Mairead, Cailean, Ewan, Kila," he said, nodding to each one as he said their names, "are my younger siblings. Ye already ken Duncan and Griogair."

"Hello," she said.

His siblings were silent and watched her as if she spoke a foreign language.

Darra paled and blinked, obviously affected by their rudeness.

"That is nay way tae treat our guest," Rory said, giving them a fierce frown.

His reprimand pulled them out of their stupor. Mairead murmured her greeting first, her cheeks stained with embarrassment. The others followed suit, mumbling their half-hearted salutations.

"Cailean," he said. "Show Lady Darra tae Da's bed chamber."

"Here, take this." Cailean thrust the reins to Ewan, his youngest brother. Slanting his eyes at Darra, he said, "Follow me, milady."

As soon as Darra disappeared into the main tower, Rory glared at the rest of his siblings. "Ye should all be ashamed of yourselves," he said.

"Did ye ever think tae give us some warning first before ye bring a *sassenach* tae our home?" Mairead demanded, her fists clenched at her skirt.

"Aye, ye may have nae noticed, Rory," Kila added, her voice dripping with sarcasm, "But she's English, and we dinnae like the English here." She placed her hands to her slender hips. Kila had also inherited the MacGregon temper, and her expression mirrored that of her older sister's.

But Rory wasn't in the mood to be crossed. "Lady Darra has come tae heal Da," he said through clenched teeth. "While she is here ye will give her due respect." His voice became dangerously soft. "Do ye hear me?"

The reason for Darra's presence at Tancraig Castle sunk in, and effectively deflated Mairead's anger.

"Aye, Rory," Mairead said.

Ewan nodded and averted his gaze, his expression contrite. But it was Kila who continued to show defiance. She glared at him, her lips pressed together as if she was trying her best to contain her words.

Rory flicked his wrists, his patience wearing thin. "Go and see tae your chores."

One by one they did as he ordered. He was about to pivot, and seek out Duncan and Griogair when he noticed that Kila hadn't moved from her spot.

"Why are ye still here?" he growled at her. "Didnae I tell ye tae go?"

"I saw how ye look at her," she said, ignoring his questions. She straightened to her full height and glared at him. "She may be here tae heal Da, but just because ye like her disnae mean the rest of us will." Having said her piece, she threw him a withering glance. Then tugging the surplus portion of her *arisaid* tighter around her proud shoulders, she stormed away.

***

The familiar smell of illness hit Darra as soon as she entered the dimly lit bed chamber. She followed Cailean closer to the bed and studied the man lying there.

Eanruing MacGregon's eyes were closed although he wasn't asleep. Every once in a while, a whimper of pain or distress erupted from his lips. A fire raged at the end of the chamber, and she couldn't tell whether the sweat on his forehead was from the excessive heat, or whether it was from his illness.

Cailean placed a hand on his father's shoulder, shaking it gently. "Wake up, Da," he said. "A new healer has come tae fix ye."

Eanruing's eyes, wild with a lingering fever, popped opened and focused on Cailean. "A healer?" he asked, confusion in his voice. He let out a ragged breath, and his fevered awareness settled onto Darra. "Venora...?" he said.

Hearing her mother's name startled her, but she quickly recovered from her surprise. She glanced over at Cailean, but he had no reaction. "Venora is my mother's name," she said slowly. "I am Darra."

So many questions ran through her mind. She wanted to know why and how Eanruing was acquainted with her mother. She also wanted to ask why Clan Lochclay considered them their enemy. But Eanruing wasn't lucid enough to answer any of her questions.

The older man closed his eyes just as a sudden seizure came upon him. He thrashed in his bed, his head rolling from side to side. A cry escaped from deep within his chest, and he arched his back as if a creature dug sharp talons into his back.

"I will need a basin of water and some linen," she told Cailean calmly, and set her basket on the mattress.

"Aye, I'll be right back," he said, and rushed out of the chamber.

A few minutes later, he arrived with Mairead who held a bowl of water and clean linen in her hands. Her countenance was pinched and drained of color.

Another moan emerged from Eanruing's lips, and Rory's sister rushed over to her father's bedside. "It appears that he's getting worse," she said.

"Ye need tae do something, milady," Cailean said. There was real fear in his voice. Any animosity that she sensed earlier from them was gone, and they looked to her as if she possessed the power to produce miracles. Darra didn't have magic, but she had the knowledge of herbs, roots, and their medicinal uses.

She reached for the cloth in Mairead's hand. Dipping it into the basin, she said, "Until I make my assessment, I cannot know how to help him." She wrung out the cloth and placed it on his burning forehead. "His temperature is too high." Darra glanced over at the other woman. "Have you given him anything for his fever?"

Mairead nodded slowly. "The village healer has given him many things, but I dinnae ken what they were."

Darra twisted her lips to the side. Clearly the healer's remedies were ineffective. There were hundreds of ways to treat a fever; some were more aggressive than others. She needed more time to observe him before she could decide on a remedy to try.

Digging into her medicine basket disturbed the contents, causing the faint smell of dried herbs to waft into the air. She breathed in the familiar scents. There was something about the fragrance that comforted her. From her apprenticeship, she recognized that there were multiple cures for every human complaint. Thanks to Lady Venora's teachings as well as pouring through the medicinal journals in the solar, she was able to commit a number of recipes to memory.

When her mother was laden with grief, it was Darra that people sought. All the years of learning the herbal arts made her a competent healer in her own right. It awarded her great satisfaction in helping the sick.

She saw a jug of ale and a tumbler at the table beside the bed. Bringing out a small flask of plant oil from her basket, she poured a drop into the drink. Next, she sifted through her supplies and found the small sack at the bottom of the basket. She untied the string and opened the satchel. Carefully taking a bit of the root powder, she rubbed her fingers together, dropping the dried substance into the wine, and releasing a pungent smell in the air. Darra dusted her fingers and twisted the bag closed. One pinch was enough. If she put more than that, it would give Eanruing stomach pains. She swirled the vessel, allowing the particles to dissolve into the liquid.

Satisfied with the concoction, she turned to the sickly man. He had gone still. She gently cradled his head, lifting the cup to his lips. "Open your mouth, my lord," she said.

When he did as she instructed, she pressed the cup closer to his lips and slowly tipped the healing liquid into his mouth. A portion of it spilled down his jaw, and she lifted his head higher so that the drink drained into his throat.

He began to choke just as Kila and Ewan entered the chamber.

Kila eyed the cup in her hand. "Take that away. Da disnae want tae drink that," she declared.

Mairead came to stand by her siblings. "That is enough, Kila," she said.

"'Tis all right." Darra looked up from her task. Even though the younger girl didn't say it out loud, Darra could hear the underlying fear in her voice. "This potion will bring down the fever," she explained, her tone patient. "He needs to drink all of it in order to get well."

For a moment, suspicion and indecision warred on Kila's countenance. She opened her mouth to say something, but Mairead put a hand on her arm, stopping her. "Give her a chance," she said.

Darra threw Mairead a grateful smile before continuing with her work.

"I believe that your father will recover," she said casually wiping up some of the liquid that dribbled down his chin. "Your mother should be happy to know this."

"Our mother is dead," Kila said flatly.

Darra's hand flew to cover her mouth. She had assumed that the lady of the house was busy elsewhere. It never occurred to her that she had passed away.

Mairead nudged her sister. "Lady Darra is a visitor here. She disnae need tae ken our business."

"I am sorry —"

"Dinnae concern yourself," Kila said shortly. "Just concentrate on making Da better."

Darra nodded and poured every last drop of the herbal remedy into Eanruing. Then she waited for the medicine to take its effect.

A short while later, Eanruing's eyes closed, and the sound of his deep, even breathing filled the chamber. She gently settled his head back onto his pillow and straightened her spine.

"He's sleeping," Mairead said with wonder in her voice. She brushed a damp cloth over her father's forehead, wiping away the sweat. "And his forehead feels cooler to the touch."

"Da might very well recover from his illness," Ewan added. "Since he fell ill weeks ago, I dinnae think he has slept this well."

Kila watched her father's face with some reservation. She still seemed conflicted about her feelings toward Darra, but there was no disputing that Eanruing appeared restful.

"Ewan," Mairead said, "Go tell Rory and the others that Da's fever has broken."

The youth turned to Darra before exiting the bed chamber. "Rory was right about ye, milady. It appears that ye do ken what ye are doing."

There was a noise at the door, and Darra whirled around.

"Didna I tell ye tae go —" Mairead said, and then stopped when she saw the man at the threshold. A smile surged to her lips. "Och, Blane, I though ye were Ewan. I didnae ken ye were here."

"Blane!" Kila said, rushing over and embracing him.

"I came tae see Eanruing."

"Dinnae worry, Blane," Mairead said, gesturing to Darra, "Lady Darra has healed Da of his fever!"

"'Tis a temporary cure," Darra said, smiling tiredly. "He will need to take more medicine when he wakes up."

Blane cast a skeptical glance at her. "'Tis nae wise tae trust the English," he said.

The smile on her face diminished. She felt a hot flush rise to her cheeks and the tops of her ears began to burn. She was physically exhausted from her journey, and she was fed up with the rudeness that she encountered at every turn. The man's words triggered her temper, and before she could stop herself, she said, "I am told that 'tis not wise to trust a Highlander either."

Kila gaped at her as if Darra had insulted the whole of Scotland. And she supposed she had, but she didn't care.

Darra and Blane stared at one another, each person not willing to relent. His eyebrows snapped down, and hatred spit from his eyes. If Darra wasn't a woman, she was certain that he would have punched her.

Finally Mairead stepped in between them. "We should leave this bed chamber, and convene in the great hall," she said, taking Darra by the arm and leading her out of the small room. Instinctively Rory's younger sister seemed to know that the situation was starting to become volatile and she wanted to stifle it. "Da needs tae rest, and Lady Darra must be starving from her long journey."

Darra allowed herself to be led away. As she walked, she could feel Blane's stare boring into her back.

"Your father should be well in a few days," she told Mairead, trying to ignore the unsettling sensation. "My understanding is that I will be allowed to return home once my work is done. But before I go, I will leave a bottle of the tincture with you."

Mairead nodded and smiled as if she was relieved that Darra didn't mean to stay long.

A lump formed in Darra's throat. And the elation of successfully treating a patient faded quickly. She had to stay a few more days, but she desired to leave Tancraig Castle immediately. Under the thin veil of truce, she was well aware of the simmering hostility directed at her. She didn't belong in the highlands, and it was a misjudgment to come here in the first place.

Chapter 12

❧❧

Eanruing MacGregon heard a whispering noise at the side of his bed and with effort, he moved his head to see who was there. His poor heart thumped hard in his chest as he took in the angelic creature.

Venora.

But then the lass turned, and he saw that he was wrong; it wasn't Venora after all but her daughter. The lass was as charming and fair as her mother. She had the same pale, smooth complexion and flaxen hair.

He breathed in slowly, the images of his youth flashing through his mind. He was a braw lad at the time, and he had the lassies hovering around him like bees to a flowering plant. In truth, he had the pick of any lass from the neighboring clans, but he cared for none of them. That was until he met Venora Lochclay. She was a noblewoman, the niece of the laird of Balhain. And she had the rare ability to relate to common and noble folks.

He first saw her at a village fair, and he immediately drawn to her beauty. Later he learned that she visited the town often with her father to peddle their herbal potions at the market square, and to treat the sick. Eanruing became acquainted with her father, Robart Lochclay, and learned that he was a man who practiced medicinal arts. A way to win the lass was to go through her father, so he befriended Robart while he plied his charms on Venora.

When his wee brother became sick, he felt fortunate in his friendship with Robart, and sought his help. Lochclay came immediately. And after examining Jonat, he began to mix a variety of powders and dried substances into a cup of ale, substances that Eanruing had never seen or smelled before. It was foul stuff. Not surprisingly, the bairn fought and screamed as if a wild boar attacked him. It was surprising how strong the lad was, considering he only had five summers behind him.

"Hold him down," Robart commanded.

"Nay!" Jonat wailed. "I dinnae want it!"

Eanruing looked over at his mother. Her face was devoid of color, but when she caught his eye, she nodded her head in consent.

He moved to secure the lad while Robart poured the liquid down his gullet.

It should have ended happily, but the lad began coughing uncontrollably.

Sweat formed over his own forehead, and he heard the heavy thud of his heart. "Is this normal?" he asked.

Robart blinked at him, a panicked look in his eyes. He raised his arm to wipe his forehead. "Nay, 'tis an unusual reaction."

The coughing went for long minutes, and his brother turned purple. Robart tried to give the lad more of the medicinal drink, but Jonat ended up spewing it into the air. Each cough wracked his poor frame until finally, his thrashing body stilled and his coughing ceased.

Eanruing relaxed his grip on his brother. At first he was glad that Jonat had fallen asleep, but then he sensed that something was wrong. He bent down to inspect Jonat.

"He isnae breathing," he said.

His mother gasped. She ran to Jonat's side, grabbing the lad and shaking him by the shoulders. "Jonat, wake up!" she yelled.

Eanruing studied the other man, his blood starting to boil. "What did ye give the lad?"

"'Tis a common formula for — for pneumonia," he said, backing away.

"Ye murderer," Eanruing shouted. "Ye killed the wee bairn!"

"Nay," he shook his head adamantly. "He reacted badly tae the drink —"

But everything around Eanruing grew red, and he couldn't see or hear anything else. A rage so dark filled his entire being. He already lost his father, and Jonat was too young to die.

The fury inside him grew to a fever pitch, and he drew his blade from his belt. But as he stalked toward the other man, his foot stubbed on a crack on the floor, and he pitched forward, falling hard onto the healer.

A screamed sounded.

When Eanruing recovered, he saw a blotch of red on his tunic, and his hands were covered with blood.

Lochclay stared at him, horror and shock frozen on his countenance. At the same time, his hands clutched at the dirk that jutted out from his chest. A gurgling emerged from his lips and he collapsed onto the ground.

His mother screamed and screamed, the sound reverberating throughout the small bed chamber.

Eanruing staggered back, staring at the corpse sprawled on the floor. The back of his leg bumped into a wooden chair and he sat down heavily on it.

"What did ye do, lad?" his mother cried, her palms framing her tear stained countenance. Fear, worry and panic were betrayed in her eyes.

The words wouldn't come out, and all he could do was shake his head. He had only wanted to scare Lochclay, not kill him.

He buried his face in his blood stained hands, trying to block out the image of the dead man in his home. But Robart's shrill scream continued to ring in his ears, and the unmistakable metallic odor of blood permeated the bed chamber.

Eanruing didn't know how long he sat in the chair, but it was his mother who roused him from his shocked stupor.

"Ye will need tae tell them about what happened," she said, her voice devoid of emotion. "Ye need tae tell Laird Balhain that ye didnae mean tae kill his brother, that 'twas an accident."

And he did tell them, only Edwin Lochclay went into a rampage, declaring war on the MacGregons.

The MacGregons fought hard and valiantly, killing as many men as they lost. But the loss took its toll on his people, and the widows cried for him to stop the fighting.

The Laird of Balhain refused to listen to reason, so Eanruing came up with an idea to end the skirmish once and for all. It was a desperate attempt, but it was worth a try. He sought Venora out at the town market, hoping to win her to his side. With her help, he believed that she could convince her uncle that it was all a misunderstanding, that Robart's death was accidental. Except the lass refused to speak with Eanruing.

On a third attempt to talk with her, he discovered that she had vanished. All hope of ending the war was gone. After her disappearance, the warfare between the two clans intensified, becoming more bloody and brutal with each passing day. Even at present, the hatred between the clans simmered as hotly as if the tragedy occurred yesterday.

Eanruing let out a sigh, not wanting to think about the terrible past.

He felt someone at his side. Focusing his eyes, he found Darra peering down at him. Her hand was close to his and he reached for it, thankful for a respite from his dark recollections. She gasped and jerked out of his grasp.

His hand hung in mid-air, and for a brief moment, he had a chance to really observe the ugly limb. The skin was pulled taut over the knuckles, and it appeared foreign, as if it belonged to someone else. More than anything, it appeared like a claw rather than a hand, and it trembled slightly. But Eanruing recognized it as his own because holding it up used so much of his strength.

He dropped his hand onto the bed. Never had he felt so weak, so drained. Perhaps it was because he understood that death was near. For many months, he had been sick, but it was only recently that the illness took a foothold. Tears blurred his vision, and guilt ate away at his soul. He was a man damned to hell. The one way to redeem himself was to apologize to Venora, and possibly procure her forgiveness.

But Venora wasn't here to forgive him. He was saddened to know that he would go to his grave without making amends to the woman who he wronged.

Apparently in his feverish haze, he had called out her name. And when Rory heard it, he set out to bring the lass back to the highlands. It was not surprising that she had refused to come here. She likely hated him. And for good reason. But he was a different man then — cocky, ruthless, fearless and foolish. He cared little about anyone but himself. And as the newly appointed Chief of Clan MacGregon, he believed that he was invincible.

Darra walked slowly to him, concern in her clear blue depths. She carried her basket of remedies and set it down on the mattress. Her presence at his bedside brought back painful, harsh memories that slammed into his gut, and took his breath away. His throat constricted as he tried to shut out the guilt and sorrow. A sudden thought occurred to him. Perhaps by confessing to Venora's daughter, he could be absolved of these awful feelings that gnawed at his gut. If he was going to disclose his secret, he needed to do it now — before death snatched him away.

"I want tae apologize," he said, his voice sounding rusty and disused.

Darra placed a cool hand to his forehead.

"There is no need to apologize, Eanruing," she said, her voice slow and soothing, a voice that was too similar to her mother's. "You are burning up again."

She reached over to the dressing table and brought the wine over for him to drink.

He pushed it away except she placed her hand firmly on his, holding it down. "Nay, you need to drink this."

Eanruing shook his head impatiently, but in the end she managed to get him to drink the entire contents of the cup. She set the vessel aside.

"You should get some rest."

"I cannae rest now," he said.

"Why?" she came closer to the bed and caught the edge of his blanket. "Would you like me to take off one of these furs?"

"Nay, ye dinnae understand. I'm tae blame for all that your mother has lost," he said. *All that ye have lost.*

She paused in drawing back the bed cover. "The only thing that my mother has lost is my father."

The revelation made his heart skip a beat. Venora was a widow now, he realized.

"Nay," he said, his fingers curling over the blanket. "She had lost someone else — her father."

"Aye, he died before I was born," she said, her eyebrows were drawn together in puzzlement. "You need to rest. I fear that the fever is making you delirious."

He smiled grimly. She didn't understand. Likely Venora neglected to tell her child about the role that he played in destroying her family.

"I'm sorry…" he said, his voice starting to slur. He felt the medicine taking its effect, causing a leaden weight to fall over his eyes. He hoped to clear his conscience before he passed on, except all his efforts were thwarted and the words stuck on the tip of his heavy tongue…

Chapter 13

"Ye should come tae the *ceilidh*," Mairead said, her face flushed with excitement. "'Twould be most fun."

At Darra's questioning look, Mairead's smile widened. "We come together tae celebrate summer's end, and tae give thanks for our bountiful harvest," she explained. "Every year we host a gathering in the plains where we race horses, dance, sing, and feast." She lifted her basket which was laden with breads and cakes. "'Tis our last chance tae enjoy the weather before the cruel winter covers us with its rude, icy blasts. Ye should come with us."

"I think I would be more comfortable if I stay within the castle grounds," Darra said, allowing a cautious smile to flit across her lips. The last thing she wanted was to dampen the other woman's spirits. Ever since Eanruing started to recover from his fever, his children were friendlier toward her, although she perceived that they were likely offering a fragile truce. Still, it was Mairead who made the greatest effort toward Darra.

Mairead hooked her arm around hers and led her to the window overlooking the meadow.

"See? The weather is braw," she arched a delicate brow at her. "Ye cannae stay here and be cooped up in this damp castle while the others are breathing in the fresh scent of mountain thyme and blooming heather. 'Tis a sure way tae spoil your day."

Darra chewed at the bottom of her lip. It did sound much more appealing to spend time enjoying the sunny outdoors.

Then as if she sensed the tiny resistance within Darra, Mairead smiled and pressed on. "Ye have been working hard tae help my da. Ye need a rest. What guid are ye tae him if ye are tired and cannae help him further? Besides, he is asleep now, and a servant will attend him if 'tis necessary."

"All right, you have convinced me." She sighed, and smiled back. "I shall go — but only for a little while. I shall return, and will relieve the servant so she can join in the revelry as well."

Mairead clapped her hands. "Ye will nae regret it!"

***

Darra took in the breathtaking sight before her. It was the first time that she had taken a close study of the landscape since she arrived in the highlands. The beauty was evident from afar, but standing in full view of the misty mountains, she felt humbled. The land was covered in lush, colorful vegetation, and the smell of the blooming heather filled her senses. She could very well believe that the fairies danced among the flower blossoms once the sun set behind the mountains.

Mairead led her to the outskirts of the gathering. "We'll leave our horses here with the rest," she said, gesturing to the cordoned area where a number of horses stood.

As Darra waited for Mairead to finish securing the horses, she looked awkwardly toward the crush of people. When she discovered that no one watched her, she allowed herself to relax and enjoy the sights. Children and animals alike ran about in the open field, their laughter and shouts ringing with joy and excitement. The men gathered in groups to share their drinks and conversed with great animation, while the women were busy preparing food at various cooking stations.

Mairead returned a minute later, and grabbed Darra's hand. "Let's go," she said, and pulled her into the crowd.

Darra had only taken two steps when her heart lurched at seeing Rory's strapping figure. Almost as if he sensed her presence, he twisted his head and caught her gaze. Speaking to the man beside him, he excused himself and made his way over to her. He moved with forceful grace, each stride a show of dominance and vigor. It was obvious that he was in his own element.

"Milady," he said, taking a gallant bow. Then turning to his sister, he nodded, "Mairead."

"Och, 'tis guid that ye came over, Rory." Mairead said, her voice harried and distracted. "Will ye take Darra, and show her around? I will need tae help the lassies with the food preparation."

Before Rory could respond, his sister was off.

"There is a lot tae see. Let me show ye," he said, taking her hand and placing it at the crook of his arm.

"What is *she* doing here?" a man said loudly as they passed by a group of men in their cups. He stood up and with hands at his thick waists, he scowled at her.

As if sensing violent entertainment, a number of revelers stopped what they were doing, and drifted over to them. Darra blinked rapidly, regretting that she had agreed to come to the harvest festival. She pulled the *arisaid* tighter around her shoulders even though the sun warmed her back. She should have listened to her instincts, and stayed within the castle walls. The thing she feared the most was unfolding in front of her.

"Are ye nae English, lass?" another man asked.

Her response froze in her brain as she sensed the rancor in his tone. Perhaps it was the way that she carried herself, or maybe there was an air around her which they detested. In either case, it was clear that they despised everything about her.

"It disnae matter where Lady Darra is born, Duff," Rory said, coming to her rescue.

"We cannae trust a *sassenach* in our midst," Duff said stubbornly. "What if she reports us tae our enemies?"

A murmur went through the crowd, their voices echoing with disapproval. She felt their curious scrutiny, as if they were trying to ascertain the appearance of a traitor. Her hand on Rory's arm tightened, and she wished that she could disappear into the ground.

"Duff, she willnae report ye for your cattle thievery, if that 'tis what ye are worried about," Rory said, his tone light.

"'Tis nae cattle thievery that he's worried about, Rory," another voice called out from the crowd. "'Tis the sheep, and what he does tae them that he disnae want reported."

Duff snorted, and let out a barking laugh. "Aiya, Baldie, I ken ye are jealous of my sheep."

Everyone burst out laughing.

"All right," Rory said, chuckling, "Ye have had your fun, now go back tae your games." The amiable crowd broke away, and the music started up again.

"I'm sorry that ye had tae witness that," Rory said. "Truly, a *ceilidh* is full of merriment."

"I am certain that 'tis merry," she said, giving him a wane smile.

"Ah, I see that ye remain unconvinced." He placed his large hand on her cold one. The abrupt contact sent an electric tingle through her, and she looked to see if he felt it as well, but his attention was caught by a set of dancers. "Let's watch the dancing."

She allowed herself to be dragged to the circle of people gathered together, clapping, shouting, and laughing. All the while the sounds of the bagpipes mixed in with the gleeful energy.

A couple stood across from each other, one arm each raised in an arch. When the bagpipes started in on a new melody, they began to hop gracefully from one foot to another. Darra watched as a woman approached, hooked Rory by the arm, and pulled him into the festivities. He looked at her, shrugging almost in apology before joining the reel.

The bystanders began to howl and stomp their feet to the musical beats. Meanwhile the dancers leaped with skill and agility until finally, the pipes released one loud squeal, ending the song. A grin spread across Rory's handsome face. He was making his way back to her when his youngest brother let out a shout.

"Rory, do the sword dance," Ewan said, his voice rising above the revelry. The crowd latched onto his enthusiasm and began to yell "Rory, Rory!" The tumult became deafening.

A young, pretty woman broke free from the whistling and hollering crowd, and came over to them. The lass glanced curiously at her before turning her adoring smile on to Rory. A strange pang twisted in Darra's chest. Likely when she returned home, Rory would take this woman as a wife, and forget about her.

The comely woman grabbed his hand and began to lead him away. But he dug his heels into the ground and glanced back at Darra.

"Will ye be all right?" he asked.

"Of course," she lied. "You should go. Everyone is waiting for you to dance."

He sent her a smile that went straight to her heart. She had fallen in love with him, she realized. But because of who she was, she could never have him. She blinked quickly, trying to get a hold of herself. Rory's father was close to being cured of his illness, and she would soon be released from her debt. For now, she would enjoy the celebrations, and when she went back to England, she would have something to reminisce about.

With that decision, she set aside her depressing thoughts, and allowed the festival's joyous energies to lift her spirits.

Rory moved to the front of the throng, and stood while the people applauded wildly.

Across from her, the young woman who had pulled Rory into the crowd earlier, watched him with her hand at her breast, her lovely face shining with reverence.

A man brought over two swords and crossed them on the ground.

Rory bunched his fists and placed them on his lean hips. With his back straight and his broad shoulders squared, he stretched his corded neck, tilting his chin proudly in the air. His vision focused on the distant mountains. He paused in this position for a breathless moment, showcasing his fine, muscular form. When the first poignant peal of bagpipes began, he bent at his hips and took a deep bow.

The wailing pipes echoed in the open space, mingling with the rapid, steady clapping of the onlookers. The thin strain of music started off slowly at first and then like fire, it caught on, and the tune became louder, faster. Raising his muscular arms, he arched them over his head, while holding them firm and still. At the same time, his nimble feet flashed, as he jumped, circled and leaped over, and around the sword in a powerful display of agility and male strength. There was an air of masculine poise and wildness about him, an air that was reminiscent of a raging storm gathering strength and power over the open sea.

The clan members tapped their feet and banged their hands in time to the constant rhythm which vibrated into the atmosphere. A couple of women near her sighed at the sight of such masculine magnificence, while some others around her shouted, egging Rory onward.

Somehow the skirl of the bagpipes crossed the barriers of her heart, stirring long forgotten emotions that were locked there.

"What dance is this?" she asked Ewan, who stood beside her. He was bobbing his head enthusiastically in time to the steps. She had never seen or heard of dancing with swords, and this wondrous display intrigued her.

The boy glanced over at her, his youthful countenance shining with excitement and awe. He was so caught up in observing the dance that he failed to remember his hostility toward her.

"'Tis a battle dance," he said loudly so he could be overheard above the noise. "Long ago the Scottish Prince Malcolm defeated Macbeth. 'Twas said that after his conquest, he crossed his sword with that of the slain Macbeth, and danced around them in triumph."

It was then that she realized that Rory had transformed into the Scottish Prince. His supple movements conjured images of a great ruler who had at long last conquered his mortal enemy. Malcolm's feelings of elation and triumph were captured by the quick, forceful, and precise movements of Rory's feet. Every intricate step exuded power and strength. Not once did his deft feet touch the dangerous weapons on the ground.

Every once in a while a loud, bold battle cry burst from his lips and his feet increased in speed. The hem of his great kilt flared in the air, exposing flashes of brawny thighs. Meanwhile his pointed feet landed on the ground with lethal precision, crisscrossing the double swords. He was magnificent. He was raw male energy and fluid strength. Every move he made was a show of predatory skill and tight control. Meanwhile the crowd, ever clapping to the music's tempo, incited Rory onward, joining him in his victory.

The frenzied skirl of bagpipe music resonated in sky, and her heart raced in tandem to the excitement and jubilation that he exuded.

The pipes came to a crashing halt. And the dance was over.

Rory bent at his waist in a graceful bow while the crowd cheered.

He looked over at her, holding her attention for a split second before giving a good natured laugh, and accepting the congratulations of those around him.

The swords were taken away, and the energetic shrill of bagpipe music filled the air anew. The pretty lass ran to Rory, pulling at his arm to join her in another spirited reel. But he smiled and said something to the maiden. And in a surprising move, he made his way back to Darra. The woman pouted, her gaze fixed on Rory's retreating back. She then turned an icy glare at her.

Darra let out an unsteady breath. At every turn, she seemed to make enemies. The exuberance she experienced during Rory's dance abruptly vanished, and she was once again reminded that she was an outsider and not welcomed here.

The dancing was back in full swing, where clusters of his clansmen and their ladies jumped and twirled to the high, animated strains of the pipes.

"Would ye care tae dance with me, lass?" Rory asked, offering his hand.

A pretty blush stained Darra's smooth skin. "Nay, I do not know how to dance like you do," she said almost regretfully. "Besides, I will need to go back to the castle. Your father is due to take his tincture soon."

He opened his mouth to persuade her to stay, but the expression on her pretty face was guarded. No amount of coaxing would sway her.

"Fine," he said. "I will escort ye back tae the castle."

She appeared as if she was going to decline his offer when he put up his hand. "Nay, dinnae refuse me," he said. "'Tis the least I can do after all that ye have done for Eanruing." On impulse, he reached over and ran the back of his finger along her silky cheek. "I have nae told ye that I appreciate your help with my da. Thank ye."

"You are welcome," she said, "I have long been a healer, and am glad when I can help those who suffer."

Her soft blue eyes stared up at him, and he felt something shift between them. The noise and chatter that surrounded them ceased to exist. It was almost as if he was a lad once again, clamoring for his first kiss with a bewitching lass. Her pink lips parted slightly and he was sorely tempted to dip his head and taste again from her honeyed lips. He wanted to lay her down amongst the heather, and have her groaning his name. The image caused that part of him to stir. Rory shifted uncomfortably on his feet. He needed to leave the *ceilidh* before he had a full cockstand and he embarrassed himself.

"I'll take ye tae your horse," he said, clearing his throat. His large hand engulfed her cold one, and she allowed him to lead her away. As they left the gathering and approached the area where the horses were cordoned off, the noise behind them faded.

Rory discerned that his clan members disliked her, yet he felt a strange urge to protect her from their hostilities. For such a delicate lass, she impacted him in ways that he couldn't understand. And as much as he tried to push her away from him, he gravitated back to her. She demonstrated that not all English folk were terrible. Some of them could be kind and caring — like Darra. The disturbing thing was that he no longer minded that she was an English woman. Still, she was intent on going back to her homeland, and he promised to release her once she fixed Eanruing. But why didn't he want her to leave?

Chapter 14
❧

The grounds of Tancraig Castle were quiet since most of the inhabitants were still at the *ceilidh*.

They maneuvered the horses into the stable, and Rory helped Darra dismount. He deliberately slid her body down along his compact frame until she stood facing him.

"I missed ye," he said, reaching out to touch her soft skin. Suddenly the recollections of the night they shared hit him like a gale force. And despite himself, his body reacted to the tantalizing memories. He longed to rebury himself in her sheath and stay there.

Her eyes widened with confusion. "I — I do not understand. You were with me all this time…"

Mairead had lent her an *arisaid*, which she had pulled over her shoulders to cover the fitted shift and kirtle underneath. By all accounts, she looked like she belonged in Scotland. And by god, he could so easily get lost in her pretty blue eyes. All at once, Rory was overcome with an urge to kiss her. He grabbed her lightly by the wrist, his surprising movement taking her off guard. Then pushing her to the stable wall, he pinned both arms above her head.

She didn't resist him, but instead regarded him with a mixture of excitement, wariness and curiosity.

If she was frightened by him, he would have released her immediately. However she was staring at his mouth now, her breath coming out in spurts. He could feel his shaft thickening under his kilt, aching to probe her velvet softness.

He pushed his hips forward, allowing her to feel his hardness.

"I want ye, lass," he said, his voice gruff.

Her pupils darkened as if she too remembered that night that they made love. But then she looked over his shoulder and licked her lips nervously. "The men —"

"Willnae be back for a time," he finished for her, and bent to softly nip at the bottom of her luscious lip. He dragged his mouth until they covered hers, taking in her sweetness. She stiffened at his initial touch, but subsequently her body softened under the tender assault.

His hands lifted to the soft plaid on her shoulders and slid it off, exposing the bare skin above her bodice.

"Such a bonny sight," he breathed.

His hands skimmed across her flushed skin, down her upper arms, and sliding over to the swell of her fitted bodice. Through the fabric he cradled her breasts with his palms, first testing the weight of them, and then gently swirling his thumbs over the hardening nubs. She arched her back and let out a low moan that was filled with desire, a desire that echoed his own.

"And ye smell sae guid," he murmured, breathing in the fresh floral scent, and the smell of woman. She leaned her head on the wooden panel behind her as if she needed it for support. His blistering lips trailed to her neck, finding the sensitive spot there and nipping softly at it. She jerked forward, her breasts mashing against his chest. He shifted her slightly to dip his head, licking a scorching wet trail along her collarbone and down to the valley between her swollen breasts.

"Rory," she moaned, reaching to place her palms on his shoulders.

The sound of his name caused his bollocks to tighten and his cock to jump.

He growled, moving up to capture her lips. Raising her leg, he wrapped it around his waist, making it potently clear that he wanted her. His hand dropped down to cup her buttocks, lifting her until her sex cradled his erection. He groaned at the exquisite softness and circled his hips, wanting to get closer to her, in her.

Rory started to tug up her gown when he paused. Frantic shouts and flying hooves outside the stable filled his ears and instantly cooled his ardor.

He allowed the fabric to drop and pulled Darra away from the stable wall. Her eyes fluttered open, and in the dim light of the stable, it glittered with confusion.

"Someone's calling out your name, lass," he said.

***

Darra blinked as her eyes adjusted to the bright light outside of the stable. A rider along with a horse and cart was careening toward the keep. The horseman twisted his head and saw them standing at the stable. Jerking at his reins, he caused the horse to lean back on its hind legs, its front legs pawing in the air. The horse's whinny filled the courtyard. When the animal settled its hooves back onto the ground, the rider whirled the beast around, urging it toward the wooden structure. The horse and cart behind him made a wide circle, following the rider in his new course.

She raised her hand to shield her eyes from the sun, and as the horseman came closer, she said in surprise, "Why, 'tis Cailean."

Before long, Cailean halted in front of them and scrambled down from the horse. "'Tis fortunate that we dinnae have tae search for ye in the keep," he said, his breath coming out harshly. He gestured to the cart behind him. "There's been an accident."

The horse and cart came to an abrupt stop.

Darra shifted to the side to get a clear view of the transport. As the man in the driver's seat looked down at her, she recognized him. It was Duff, the man who had ridiculed her at the harvest festival. But there was no animosity in his regard, only desperation. Before she could question why he was here, she heard a woman weeping at the back of the cart.

Darra moved quickly to the wooden contraption while Cailean and Rory trailed after her.

The woman glanced up at her approach, her face streaked with tears. A child about four years old lay in her lap, his small arms cradling his stomach.

"Please, milady," the woman said, a sob in her voice. "Help us. He's all that we have."

She nodded. "I will need my healing basket," she said.

"I'll get it for ye," Cailean said. Jumping back onto the horse, he raced toward the keep to retrieve her supplies.

"I will need to know what happened," she said, turning to assess the boy's demeanor. His skin was flushed, and soft mewling cries escaped intermittently from his lips.

"I went tae get some food from the sharing table when I heard yelling," the woman replied. "When I spun around tae see what all the commotion was about, Duff was carrying my wee Allie tae me." She let out a loud sniff. Reaching into a pouch that hung at her belt, she pulled out three bright red berries. "Some bairns said that they saw the lad eating these."

Darra's blood ran cold as she peered at the yew berries in the other woman's hand. The ruby flesh were edible, but the seeds inside were potent enough to kill a grown man.

She bent down and touched the boy's burning forehead. "How many berries did you eat, Allie?"

"One," he said, lifting up a small finger.

"Aye," Duff confirmed, coming to stand next to his wife and child. "The other bairns said the lad tried tae eat another berry, but they knocked it out of his hands."

"You will be fine," Darra said, patting Allie gently on the head. Straightening up, she looked at his parents. "One fruit will not kill him. Do you know if he retched after eating it?"

"Aye," the woman said, hope filling her eyes. "He did a wee bit at the *ceilidh*."

"Is this significant?" Duff reached down to hold his wife's hand, the same hope reflected on his rough countenance.

"'Tis good that he vomited the poison, however we need to make certain that all of it is removed from his gut," she explained.

The rumble of hooves sounded off in the distance. Cailean had returned with her supplies. He reared his horse and quickly dismounted.

"Here ye go," he said, panting as he handed her the medicinal basket.

Darra nodded her thanks, and sifted through the contents. Her fingers closed around a small flask of wine and a satchel of fig tree ash. Pulling the items out, she carefully dropped some of the ash into the liquid and closed the lid.

"He will need to drink this medicine," she said, shaking the bottle to mix it. "It will help him expel the rest of the poison."

"He disnae like tae drink much of anything, but I will make him take it," Duff said, his Adam's apple bobbing up and down.

Darra gave him a reassuring smile and shook her head. "'Tis not necessary," she said, and turned her focus back to the young boy. He was a healthy lad, and after he emptied his stomach of all traces of the poison, he would recover quickly. Without a doubt he would be running around in the town square with his friends within the next day or so.

"Allie, I need your help," she said.

The boy looked at her warily. "Help ye with what?"

"I need you to show your Chief and your da how brave you are," she paused. "Do you think you can you do that?"

"Aye," he rubbed his belly and whimpered. "But it hurts."

"I know it does." She showed him the bottle. "Do you see this? This medicine will not taste very good, and it will make you a little ill, but if you take it, you will feel better. Do you want to feel better, Allie?"

He nodded again although this time his response was much slower.

"That is a fine lad," she said smiling. "Now sit up and open your mouth."

The boy's gaze flicked from his father to Rory, and then he reluctantly opened his jaw. Seizing the moment before he changed his mind, she tipped a portion of the concoction into his mouth and he dutifully swallowed it.

A few seconds later, he began to cough, and the rest of the contents of his stomach emptied.

When the boy was finished, he nestled against his mother and went to sleep. Soon his breathing was even and steady.

Darra touched his forehead again, and while she found it warm, it wasn't burning as before. Dropping her hand to her side, she said, "The fever should be gone by the time he wakes up."

The woman lifted her fingers to wipe at the dampness on her cheeks. "Thank ye, milady. Ye are an angel, a blessing."

"Aye, thank ye milady." Duff pulled at his collar and his face reddened slightly. "I'm sorry for saying those things at the *ceilidh*…"

"'Tis of no consequence," she waved her hand, dismissing his words. "I have already forgotten it."

Relief flooded his face and he gave her a broad grin. "Unlike the village hag, ye ken what ye are doing," he said. "Now we have someone we can rely on." He clapped Rory on the back. "'Tis a guid thing that ye brought the lass here."

Rory placed an arm over her shoulder and smiled down at her. "Aye, the lass is a boon tae us."

She brushed at the strand of hair that fell across her forehead, embarrassed and pleased at being the focus of attention. The boy was going to be all right, and she had a hand in making that possible. Darra prided herself in understanding how to combine the power of herbs and roots, and assisting people with their healing. She loved to help people. But then in the next moment her elation deflated, and she recalled she had yet to heal one person — Eanruing MacGregon.

Chapter 15

❦❧

Rory leaned against the old oak tree, his arms folded over his chest as he watched Darra crouched at the ground, digging for Gaiaroot. He knew that he should offer to help her, but he was loathed to leave his post. At the moment, he had a good view of the slopes of her breasts, and he rather enjoyed the angle.

She looked up. "Thank you for bringing me here, Rory," she said, sending him a sunny smile.

The smile hit him in the solar plexus. "Ye are welcome," he said.

The sight of her captivating visage made the air catch in his gullet. Her oval face was so perfectly formed, her eyes as blue as the deep ocean. And her pink lips were as alluring as the day that he first he saw them. He felt the familiar urge to kiss her. Since their night in the woods, he dreamed of her, yearning to feel, touch and taste her sweet body. Then there was that moment in the stables yesterday. If they weren't interrupted, they would have enjoyed a passionate spell in each other's arms.

Darra lifted a hand and wiped at her brow. She happily surveyed the flowering heather which spanned the horizon.

"The Gaiaroots are so abundant here among the heather," she explained. "Mairead brought me to this spot once to gather thyme, but I discovered these miracle plants. I never knew that they grew in the highlands." She went back to her digging. "And 'tis fortunate how easily I can replenish my supply."

Darra continued with the medicinal virtues of the root, and how it could treat fevers, wounds, sore throats, and a host of other internal ailments. But he could scarcely concentrate on the stream of information when all he wanted was to take a strand of her silky golden hair, place it under his nose and breathe in her sweet womanly perfume.

He ached to feel her again.

Rory pushed away from the tree and approached her.

"My medicine book at home…" She paused in her digging, her voice trailing off as she spied his boots in front of her. Slowly she looked up, settling her regard on his visage.

"Is there something wrong?" she asked, a delicate brow raised in puzzlement.

A streak of energy shot through him as he took her hand, pulling her up from the ground. She felt the disturbance as well because she dropped the dagger in her hand. Darra stared at him as if he had somehow hexed her. But it was really she who bewitched him.

"There is nay one here but the two of us," he said, reaching to touch her cheek, caressing the smooth, creamy skin. He remembered that the rest of her body was as soft, as lovely, and he wanted to plunge himself into her.

Her eyes darkened with barely suppressed hunger, and she licked her lips nervously. "What do you —?"

He shook his head, cutting her off. "We need tae finish what we started in the stable," he said, his hot gaze roving over her curves.

A flush stained her cheeks and she bent her head.

"Nay, lass, dinnae look away from me," he commanded softly.

Darra dragged her eyes from the ground. But then her attention became riveted to the sizable bulge beneath his great kilt.

When he was satisfied that he had Darra's full attention, he lifted up his kilt to display his arousal, which was standing erect and proud. Even though she had seen him before, she allowed herself to study him with unabashed fascination. And he was as breathtaking as she remembered. Still, it was difficult to fathom how his entire shaft had entered her. But somehow it did.

"Do ye like what ye see, lass?" he murmured. His hand gripped his cock, and he began to stroke the rigid appendage.

At his question a streak of heat zipped through her entire frame. She wet her lips, but she was unable to speak.

One corner of his mouth quirked at her loss for words. With his muscular legs wide apart, he continued to knead the flanged head of his cock. She didn't know if it was her imagination, but he seemed to grow bigger the longer she ogled him.

But then it seemed that he had enough of playing. Dropping his hand, he moved until he stood an arm's length away. The intense heat that radiated off his muscular build made her take a step back and she bumped into the oak tree.

Placing a hand on the tree trunk, he bent his head. "In case ye didnae notice, lass, ye drive me mad with desire for ye," he said, his hot breath brushing across her temple.

He brought one hand to cup her face, capturing her lips in a lush kiss that was laced with need, want, and primal hunger.

The intensity of the contact sparked a moment of shock to her system, but then little by little, her body began to yield, to melt against his solidness. It seemed to know that this was where it belonged, where it wanted to stay.

Darra placed her palms at the sides of his face, kissing him back. Sparks flew with every press of her lips. At first he held still, allowing her to leisurely explore his sculpted lips. But then he had enough.

His strong arms wrapped around her hips, drawing her closer until she could feel the ridge of his erection thrusting insistently against her sex. She already knew how it felt to be pleasured by him, to have that hard, firm part of him impale her.

A moan of pure desire purred in her chest. And an eagerness welled up in her belly. Suddenly she wanted him inside her. Now.

"Please, Rory," she said.

"Please what?" he murmured.

His hand went to her hair, brushing it aside so that he exposed her neck. He then buried his face at the curve of her neck, grazing his hot lips along the sensitive part of her skin.

She let out a soft whimper and tilted her head, giving him greater access. His searing touch shot straight down to her stomach. That now familiar liquid fire coiled further down until it settled at her core, making her damp.

As if he sensed the inviting heat from her sex, his sinewy arm tightened around her hips, drawing her close. At the same time, he dragged his mouth across her jaw line and settled his lips over hers. Her arms went up and circled his neck as she pressed herself closer to his rigid frame.

He slipped his tongue into her mouth while another sigh gathered deep in her throat. Just then, he pushed her gently against the tree trunk, and his large palm drifted down her leg. Hoisting the hem of her gown, he drew the material to her midriff. She vaguely noted a cool breeze brushing against her scorched skin. He raised her leg and wrapped it around his waist, pressing his throbbing member against her slick heat.

She gasped as his hips began to rock against her, the back and forth motion causing the tip of his rod to lightly stroke her moist folds. A streak of relentless anticipation coursed through her center. If it was possible, she could feel herself becoming wetter, slicker with each pass. It was pure torture. It was pure bliss.

Leaning back against the rough bark, she savored the delicious agony of his shaft rubbing along her clitoris. She thought that she would collapse from the pleasure of it.

But he stopped.

Vaguely, she felt him moving away from her as he tugged down her skirt.

"Rory?" she said as a sense of loss crashed down on her.

"Someone's coming," he said, quickly adjusting his kilt.

She looked past his shoulders, and saw Ewan riding toward them, his arm flailing in the air while he shouted Rory's name.

Her heart froze as reality hit her like a bucket of freezing water. If Rory was less alert, she would have been caught in an illicit act. What was it about him that made her lose all her faculties?

A blush rose to her cheeks as she remembered her wanton behavior. The first time they made love, she merely wanted to experience rapturous passion. But now she wanted to keep experiencing it.

Ewan jumped down from his horse and picked his way through the rocky surface, his youthful face red with exertion. When he finally reached them, he bent over at his waist, his hands braced against his knees as he tried to catch his breath.

"Mairead —" he gasped. He tried again. "Mairead said tae come get ye."

"Why?" Rory said, sharply.

"'Tis Da," Ewan said, taking a big gulp of air and gesturing toward Tancraig Castle. "His fever is back and raging worse than before."

Darra moved quickly to gather her basket. "Let us get back to the castle."

They tore across the rocky, uneven terrain, their horses' hooves kicking up clumps of heather and dirt. All the while, her mind raced. Why was Eanruing feverish again? When she had left, his temperature was stable. She had given Mairead instruction to administer the herbal tincture every three hours. Did she forget? It didn't make any sense that his fever was getting worse.

Glancing over at Rory, she saw that his face was tensed. Any trace of the playful, passionate man that kissed her was gone.

Mairead waited for them at the steps of the keep. When she saw them approaching, the worried expression on her pretty face turned to relief.

"I was uncertain whether or nae Ewan would be able tae find ye." She signaled for the stable hands to take the horses away.

"Tell me what happened," Rory said.

Mairead gave them a recount as she led them to Eanruing's bed chamber. Blane and the rest of Rory's siblings were already there.

Everyone looked at them as soon as they entered.

"'Tis all her fault," Blane said, pointing a finger at Darra. "I dinnae ken why ye brought her here, Rory. She cannae be trusted."

Her steps faltered. "But I have not —"

"I think ye have given him poison." Blane stared at everyone in the room. "Have ye ever considered that the 'medicine' that she's given tae Eanruing may nae contain the cure that she claims?"

Blane glared at her as if she was a murderess, and suddenly she was filled with righteous indignation. In all her work as a healer, she had never been blamed for harming anyone. And to be so falsely accused wounded her deeply.

"Why do you…?" Darra swallowed hard, struggling to control the anger in her voice. She tried again. "What have I ever done to make you hate me so?" she asked.

"Ye are English." He bent his head and spat on the ground as if that was all the explanation that he needed to give. But when he raised his head again, he sent her a frigid glare that chilled her to her marrow. "I *hate* the English."

She took a step back, feeling the blast of his enmity. "The English have also suffered," she said. "I have seen what you Scots have done to my people."

"'Tis nae the same!" he roared. "Your people destroyed my family." His voice shook from the brutal force of his emotion. "My home burnt tae the ground and my family in it." Unshed tears glistened in his eyes as he glowered at her. "They were innocent and harmed nay one." He blinked and his tone lowered in remembered agony. "The bastards didnae ken that I was hiding in the hills overlooking my house, watching my kin being burned alive..."

She felt the blood drain from her visage.

"I am sorry for your loss," she said, attempting to keep her voice stable as the shock of his revelation hit her. Darra didn't know what King Harold and his men did outside the English borders. She certainly had no idea that they were so brutal, so cruel.

"What do ye ken of my loss?" Blane demanded furiously. He bunched his fists at his side as if he was restraining himself from ramming them into something or someone. "Ye live in your sheltered castle while your kinsmen go out and murder guid people." The bitterness in his voice seeped into the room, affecting everyone in the vicinity.

"The lass cannae be blamed for the death of your relations," Rory said, cutting into the thick silence. "Indeed the womenfolk cannot be responsible for what their men do."

"Then ye are a fool tae believe it," Blane said bitterly. "The enemy is the enemy, whether they be womenfolk or nae." He waved at the basket in Darra's hand. "She claims tae ken how tae heal, sae she would also ken how tae kill."

"I dinnae believe it." Rory shook his head and folded his arms across his massive chest.

"Ye dinnae believe it because ye are too busy fucking your English whore," Blane said, his face darkening.

Darra drew in a sharp breath. His words lashed out at her like a whip. With everyone assessing her, she wanted to perish from the humiliation.

Rory walked up to Blane. "Dinnae call the lass that," he said, his voice dangerously soft.

"Or what will ye do, Rory?" he said, his voice tight and taunting. "Everyone kens what ye have been doing with the whore —"

Rory pulled his arm back and rammed his fist into Blane's jaw, causing the other man's head to snap back.

"I said dinnae call the lass that," he said. Turning to Darra, his expression was apologetic. "'Tis unfortunate that ye had tae hear that, lass." He appeared as if he was going to say more when he stopped abruptly, and focused on something past her shoulders. Darra whirled around, and watched in horror as Blane came throttling toward them like a rabid boar.

Reaching for her arm, Rory flung her aside just as Blane dove at him, knocking his legs out from under him. The air whooshed from his lungs and he landed flat on his back.

In the next moment, Blane was straddled on top of him, ramming Rory's face with his fists.

"Stop it!" Darra yelled. When the brawling men ignored her, she turned to the person closest to her. "Griogair, do something! Rory is getting hurt!"

Griogair started to a step forward when Duncan stopped him. "This is between Rory and Blane."

She looked at Duncan in disbelief. "You cannot mean to have the man beat on your brother!"

"Rory would nae like it if we interfered," Duncan said.

They hadn't fought like this since they were lads, but this battle was different. Blane was out for blood. He seemed to dip into his inner rage, and every slight, every torment he suffered in the hands of the English was targeted at Rory.

Fortunately Rory managed to throw in a few solid strikes, but his friend retaliated and delivered his fair share of hits.

Rory raised his forearms to avoid another punch to his head, but the impact on his arms still rattled his teeth. After several more pounding blows, he sensed that Blane was tiring, his jabs becoming slower, more sloppy.

Blane's cheek was red and swollen, and a trickle of blood ran down the side of his lip. As he threw another fist, Rory trapped it between his arms, locking onto the limb and wrenching it downward. The abrupt movement propelled Blane's torso forward, throwing him off balance.

Then calling upon his reserve, Rory lifted his hips in the air, pitched his weight to the side, and flipped them both over so that he was positioned on top.

"I bested ye when we were lads," he growled. "Today willnae be different."

With that, he rained down his fists, aiming at Blane's unprotected head. But Blane wasn't new to fighting, and he twisted his head right and left, left and right, dodging the powerful punches.

Before he understood what was happening, Blane lifted one leg up and planted his foot on Rory's chest. And with one big, violent heave, he hoisted Rory off of him.

The force of the shove hurled Rory backward, causing his arms to flail involuntarily. He spun his head around in time to see Darra, a shocked expression on her face. Why was she standing behind him and Blane? Move it, damn it! his mind screamed.

But then as if time slowed down, he felt himself hurtling in her direction, the moment of impact imminent.

And when the collision finally came, his larger form slammed into hers. She screamed. And then her body flung backward, crashing against the stone wall with a sickening thud.

She slid to the ground.

"Darra!" he cried hoarsely, clawing his way over to her and ignoring the sharp pain that shot down his back.

But when he got to her, her body was limp and lifeless.

"Nay!" he gathered her tightly in his arms, rocking her to and fro.

Mairead and Kila rushed over to his side, but he didn't want them to touch her.

Blane watched the commotion, his eyes narrowed and his chest heaving heavily. Reaching up, he wiped the blood from his mouth with the back of his hand.

"Ye shouldnae have brought her here," he said. "All ye did was tae bring trouble on our heads."

"Get out of my sight!" Rory bellowed, despair clenching at his lungs. "I dinnae want tae see your face here ever again!"

"Rory," Mairead said sharply, drawing his attention to her. "Let me see her."

Finally he nodded and allowed his sister to place her hand underneath Darra's nose. When she glanced up again, Rory saw her relief.

"She's breathing." Mairead opened her mouth to continue, but then her troubled eyes moved past Rory, and she watched as Blane retreated from the chamber. She took in a deep breath as if to compose herself before returning her attention back to Rory. "Dinnae worry, Rory," she said. "Your Darra will recover."

Chapter 16

❧❧

Your Darra will recover, Mairead's words echoed in Rory's mind. He held onto the phrase as if it was something tangible, something that he could derive comfort from. But in the end, he couldn't bring himself to believe it. The proof was right in front of him. Darra lay so still on the bed; her smooth, silken skin was pale and cool, and her breathing was barely audible.

He watched as the village healer wiped at the dried blood on Darra's temple.

"The lass cracked her head when she hit the wall," Agnes said, making a clicking noise with her tongue to demonstrate her disapproval. She slanted a look at him before going back to tend Darra's wound. "The impact was too much for such a delicate thing."

Rory nodded, and the guilt that he had unwittingly caused rose to his chest, seizing his heart and twisting it until it was hurting.

She took a bowl of herbs and peat moss, mashing the contents up with her fingers. The mixture released an acrid smell that caused his nose to twitch.

There really was no choice but to call on Agnes since he didn't know how to help Darra. The one person who would have any knowledge of healing was lying prone on the bed.

Agnes scooped a generous helping of the poultice with her fingers and applied it to Darra's temple. She then reached over to the table next to her and took a long strip of linen, wrapping the material around Darra's head.

All the while, the woman continued to make that damn sympathetic noise in her mouth. Each cooing noise reminded him of the hopelessness of the situation, and the frailness of the lovely lass that lay unconscious on the mattress. It grieved him to know that she was present only in body but not in spirit.

In his mind's eye, the scenario played over and over again, pausing and then moving in slow motion as his sizable physique slammed into her fragile form, slinging her against the uneven wall. Even now her scream echoed in his brain.

And the silence that followed gutted him. When he turned and saw her lifeless frame sprawled on the ground, his mind was seized with shock and alarm. Any anger and aggression that the fight evoked dissipated in an instant. As she lay crumpled on the ground, a sound of raw pain bellowed from his lips.

He dragged his way over to her even though he was broken and battered himself. The bastard Blane had punched him in one eye so he could only partially see Darra, but he could still recognize that her injury was severe.

Duncan moved to assist him, but he growled at his brother to move out of his way. Gently lifting her up into his arms, he took her to her bed chamber. But that was several hours ago, and here she still lay, dead to the world.

Rory's eyes traced her angelic face, willing her to wake up, willing her to view him with her alluring cobalt orbs.

"There," Agnes said, securing the linen cloth around Darra's head. The white cloth contrasted starkly against her skin, making her appear even more pale and vulnerable.

"Will she...?" He desperately wanted to ask the healer for reassurance, but the words refused to come out. Instinctively he knew what the healer would say. Yet he wanted to believe that there was at least some chance for Darra.

The healer gave him a sympathetic look, and answered his unspoken question anyhow. "There is nothing physically wrong with her — no broken bones," she made a soft click with her tongue. "It has only been three hours, my laird. Give it more time and perhaps she'll wake."

But even though she said it, he perceived that the old woman didn't believe her own words. There was a real possibility that Darra might not wake up. Everyone believed it. His siblings had come to offer support, but there was nothing they could do, and one by one they left him to his grief.

It was up to God and no one else. But Rory's faith had never been strong. Would God listen to his pleas?

After a while Agnes left the chamber, although he barely noticed. His eyes were fixed on the rise and fall of Darra's chest, grateful that she was at least breathing.

"Forgive me, lass," he whispered brokenly. With trembling hands, he reached over and smoothed a lock of hair from her lovely face. "I didnae mean to see ye hurt."

But she had no answer for him, and her silence continued to hang heavily in the air.

Rory clenched his fists together. He had saved her many times in the past. But this time was different. Everyone said that Darra's injuries were caused by the accident, but they were wrong. It was his body that flung her against the wall; he was the sole cause for her suffering. She should have awoken by now, but the devastating blow had knocked her unconscious. What would happen if she never woke up? Could he be able to live with himself? The answer that sprung to his head was an emphatic nay. He had never cared for any woman as much as he cared for Darra. And if he had to give away his life in order to save hers, he would do so without remorse. Unfortunately he was never offered an option to trade up his life.

He dropped his hand, flattening them on the mattress, and sighed.

"Wake up, my bonny lass," he said softly, reaching to cup her chin and gently shake it. When cajoling didn't work, he tightened his grip slightly, and made his tone firm and commanding. "'Tis enough, lass. Wake up, and stop trying tae put a fright in me."

But the only answering sound was the crackling of the wood burning in the fireplace.

It seemed unbelievable, but over such a short period, she managed to wedge under his skin. She made him care for her despite the fact that she was English. And the origin of her birth no longer mattered.

Rory winced when he once again remembered the audible thud against the wall. A blow like that would have felled a full grown man. He was aware that some people never woke from severe strikes to their heads.

He could feel his chest constricting and he bunched the bed-clothes in his fists. "Why did ye do it? Why did ye try tae interfere in my fight with Blane? If ye would have stayed back, ye wouldnae be hurt like this."

His questions hung heavily in the air, yet he already understood the reason why she intervened. She was a healer, and she hated to see people hurt. Except she was the one that was injured, and there was no one that could help her.

The tears burned beneath his eyelids, blurring the image he had of her. "I love ye, Darra," he said aloud, hoping that somehow she could hear him. "I dinnae ken what I'll do without ye..." He picked up her slender hand and laced his fingers with hers.

A sudden noise that arose from the courtyard seemed to make the silence in the small chamber more acute. He released her hand when he realized that he squeezed it too hard. Although he didn't know how much time passed, he determined that it was too long.

Come back, come back his mind called to her, chanting over and over again like a prayer. Folding his hands together in supplication, he raised his eyes heavenward. "God," he said, his voice pouring out in a choked half sob, "I dinnae care about myself, but take pity on the poor lass. And — and bring her back tae me."

***

A languid warmth covered Darra, a warmth that was as soft and as soothing as a summer breeze. She looked around, and was surprised to find herself in a meadow. The last thing she remembered was being in Tancraig Castle. This field seemed different somehow. The vivid color of freshly sprouted grass surrounded her, and stretched as far as she could see. Birds chirped cheerfully from the tree tops while the sound of crickets and the screech of beetles encircled her. Oddly, she felt as if she arrived early at a fairy ball, and overheard the animals and insects rehearsing their music.

Darra bent down and plucked a flower that was near her foot. She brought it up to examine its delicate petals, while her brows creased in bewilderment. Everything around her indicated that it was spring, yet she was sure that harvest time was finished, and that the leaves were now falling from their branches. How could an entire season pass without her knowledge?

Raising her gaze to the sky, she observed gray clouds curling in the distance, indicating that a storm was headed her way. But still the sun was shining overhead. It was bizarre. And though the sun shone brightly, and the trees off to her right swayed gently in the breeze, she felt no warmth, no wind kissing her skin.

Fortunately the one thing she did feel was happiness. Darra smiled, and lifted the flowering bloom to her nose, inhaling the floral scent. Since she was a little girl, she had never felt this content. But then she frowned when a sudden thought occurred to her. She scanned the meadow and discovered that the landscape now seemed strangely recognizable somehow. In fact it was similar to the area outside Lancullin Castle. Turning around, she took a staggering step back when she saw the solid castle walls looming behind her. Why didn't she notice it before?

She stepped forward, eager to return home. But she hesitated when she noticed a horseman riding across the drawbridge and heading toward the road.

Darra squinted, and when the figure became clearer, she blinked again, not believing what she saw. It was her father. There was no mistaking his solid form. He was easily the tallest man in the castle, and his height intimidated his friends and foe alike.

Excitement and delight filled her heart.

"Father!" she yelled, waving. "Here, I am over here!"

Sir Arthur Berchelaine glanced around him and slowed his horse. When he saw her, he cocked his head to one side, as if trying to discern who it was that shouted at him.

But then he recognized her and a slow grin spread across his comely face. He pivoted his horse and veered off the main road. His horse moved a short distance when it stopped abruptly. Frowning, he dismounted and tried to walk to Darra, but there was some barrier that prevented his progress.

He raised his hands and started to push at the invisible barrier. There was no give, and eventually he quit his struggles. Resting his hand on the clear wall, he began to speak.

Darra moved forward, but a similar block prevented her from getting closer.

"I cannot hear you, father. Speak louder!" she shouted.

But he continued to talk although no sound emerged from his lips. Whatever he was trying to tell her, she couldn't understand a single word.

She banged her fist uselessly against the clear barrier, a frustrated sob rising to her throat.

But then her father stopped speaking. A sadness seemed to cover him. He placed one hand over his heart, and looked at her as if he was telling her farewell.

And to her dismay, his familiar image started to waver, and slowly he along with his horse and castle began to disappear.

"Nay!" she pounded her fists furiously against the barrier. "Nay, do not leave me, father!"

But it was too late. He was gone.

Her throat tightened and she squeezed her eyes shut, feeling the tears running down her cheeks. She already lost her father, and somehow she lost him a second time.

Tiredly, she opened her eyes again. The image of her father and Lancullin Castle had completely vanished, and in their place was emptiness. She lifted her palm to beat on the invisible wall once more, but her hand passed freely through the air.

"What is —?" she gasped. And when her mind seized on the realization that the barrier was lifted, she ran to the spot where her father stood.

"Father!" she yelled, her voice echoing in the empty field.

He was truly gone. Darra sank to the ground and lay down as the sobs began to wrack her body. She had hoped with all her heart that he would reappear again, but she knew it was a useless wish. It had been so long since she had seen his smiling face. Her mother had neglected the running of the castle in her grief, and someone had to take charge and care of the inhabitants. And that someone was Darra. Stoically putting aside her own sorrow, she did what was necessary. She never admitted to anyone that she missed her father. But she did. She missed him greatly.

Darra didn't know how long she cried, how long she wallowed in her long held sadness. But slowly she became spent, and no more tears could fall. She wiped her hand across her cheek and gave a tired sigh. All the heartbreak that she had stored in her body was depleted, and now there was nothing left for her to feel.

She went on her elbows and started to push herself up when a faint voice caused her to stop.

Looking around, she couldn't pinpoint where the voice originated. Then she realized that it wasn't coming from one place but from all around. Furrowing her brows, she concentrated hard to determine what the voice was communicating. At first the words were soft and muffled, but soon it became louder, more clear — *come back, come back.*

Darra sank back down to the ground, her head resting on the soft grass. She stared up at the strange sky with the swirly clouds.

"I must be in a dream," she said to the sky.

Subsequently the clouds began to move, forming into the image of Rory MacGregor. A sudden warmth slowly filled her soul, pushing aside the last of her lingering despondency. And then she sensed love flowing all around her, through her.

Smiling, she took in a deep fortifying breath, allowing herself to fully experience the wonderful sensation.

A moment later everything changed again. She blinked rapidly, trying to comprehend what she was seeing. The green meadow had disappeared, and she now was lying on a mattress.

The smell of putrid herbs and peat filled her senses. But more than that, she felt the dull, throbbing ache at the side of her head, and she could barely contain her groan of protest.

Darra went to raise her hand and touch the bandages on her head when she paused midway, noticing that Rory sat in a chair next to her bed. His head was buried in the palms of his hands while his elbows braced against the edge of the mattress. He was so still that Darra didn't know whether he was awake or asleep.

She opened her mouth to speak, but her mouth felt as dry as a wad of fleece. Reaching over, she touched Rory's muscular forearm. The sinewy arm tensed and then twitched slightly. Slowly and cautiously, he lifted his head.

"Darra?" He stared at her as if he couldn't believe what he was seeing. But his expression quickly changed from disbelief to jubilation. "Ye are awake!" He jumped up, his sudden movement toppling over his chair. Leaning over her, he took her hands in his, drawing them to his chest. A grin filled with relief and something else spread across his striking face. "'Tis about time."

Chapter 17

ॐ∙ॐ

Venora examined Tancraig Castle as the old unpleasant feelings resurfaced. She promised herself that she would never return, yet here she was, waiting for the gates to open. While she waited, the bitterness swirled in her chest, rising higher and higher and threatening to choke her. There was nothing here except for painful memories. Her hands tightened on the reins and the horse underneath her tossed its head.

Dudley sat on his horse beside her, his patience already gone. Since he forced himself onto her party several days ago, he barely took the time to converse with her. Any interaction she had with him was through Jarin. This was fine, but truly, she wanted the knight gone from her as well. Once they were home, she would figure out a way to reverse his claim on Darra. But for now she needed to meet with the devil and his offspring.

"What is taking them so long?" Dudley said, his voice thin with irritation. His eyes scanned Tancraig Castle and a sneer formed on his lips. His vast holdings were obtained mostly from his dead wives, and this fortress likely appeared small and insignificant.

"He said that he would get Rory MacGregon —"

"I heard what the guard said." Dudely flicked his hand dismissively. "I just want to get Lady Darra and leave this shitty country."

Venora slanted her eyes at him and twisted her mouth in distaste. As much as she disliked returning to Scotland, she needed to defend the country of her birth. "If you mean to leave Scotland alive, you best not utter such disparaging remarks here."

Dudley sneered at her, and would have said something more, but a voice from above the gatehouse shouted down to them.

"What business do you have here?" the man asked.

"The guard already asked us this question," Dudley muttered angrily.

Venora ignored the knight and looked up. Squinting, she recognized the man who had held her and Fyfa hostage. She straightened her spine and gave him a cold stare. "I have come for my —"

"Betrothed," Dudley said, interrupting her. "I am here for my betrothed."

She glanced quickly at him and frowned, but he wasn't looking at her. His eyes were fixed on the younger man on the parapet.

"Hmmm," Duncan said slowly, stroking his chin. "The lass never spoke about being engaged to marry."

"That is because they are not yet promised," Venora said tightly. "Open the gates, and let us in. I want to see that my daughter is well, and that she is returned safely to me."

Almond shaped eyes that were so like his father swung over at her direction, assessing her.

"Who says that we're returning her?" he quirked an eyebrow in challenge.

Helpless anger simmered in her chest, causing her to grit her teeth. He was as arrogant as his father. If they didn't open the gates, then it would be impossible to get to her daughter. Venora refused to shelter outside the castle. It was enough that they traveled for days without bathing and other comforts. Now that they were at their destination, it was cruel for the MacGregons to leave them in the cold. This was not the highland hospitality that she was used to. She opened her mouth to reprimand Duncan when another man emerged beside him.

She gasped. It was Eanruing, but then she narrowed her eyes and saw that it wasn't him after all. It was his exact likeness; the culprit who stole Darra from her.

"Lady Venora," Rory said. "Welcome to Scotland."

She nodded in response to his greeting, but she wasn't interested in lengthy conversations over the battlements.

"I demand to see my daughter." She placed a hand on the neck of her horse to still its nervous movements. "Open the gates, if you please."

"Aye," he said. "I'll open them, but I do have one condition." His eyes swept over the guards who flanked them. "I'll allow ye tae enter, milady. The rest will have tae remain outside."

Dudley pushed forward, drawing the attention of the Highlanders. "I will be entering as well," he said, not asking for permission.

"And who are ye?" Rory asked.

"Sir Dudley, Lord of Stuham."

"I have heard about ye," he said, studying the older man.

Venora didn't particularly want to set foot in the castle without her escorts, but having Dudley at her side was better than nothing. The MacGregons had proved long ago that they couldn't be trusted. And it was a lesson she wasn't going to repeat.

"Milady?" Jarin glanced over at her, a concerned expression on his face. Clearly he didn't like the idea of her going into the castle without him, but she recognized that he would relent if she gave him the order.

"I will be fine, Sir Jarin. Then raising her voice so that Rory could hear her, she said, "I will agree to your terms. However, I require Sir Dudley to accompany me. A lady cannot go into a castle unescorted."

Silence met her request. Suddenly she began to feel a sense of dread over voicing her bold demand. What if they spurned her? In that case, she would have traveled all this way for naught.

But then Rory's voice rose, filling the air. "Open the gates!"

***

Anticipation ripped through Darra as she waited to be reunited with her mother. The excitement started as soon as Cailean had burst into her bed chamber, informing Darra and Rory that Lady Venora had arrived. Her mother could have just sent the guards, but she came herself to fetch Darra. This was significant. It would be remarkable if her mother finally broke free from her grief. There were so many things to ask her, namely why she left Scotland, and why she had never spoken about her past.

Rory gave strict orders for her to stay in bed. And while she tried to lie on the mattress, her mind raced heedlessly, and she found that it was impossible to stay still.

She walked over to the small window in her bed chamber to see if she could catch a glimpse of her mother. Unfortunately her chamber was not overlooking the courtyard, and all she could see was the mist covered mountains in the horizon.

Reaching up to her head, she winced when she touched the linen bandage. Her mother would be horrified to find her in such terrible shape. She was certain that the blame would fall on Rory's shoulders. But it was an accident, nothing more. The MacGregons treated her with kindness, and she didn't want her mother to think that she was mistreated by them.

Her nose flared slightly at the smell that followed her. She didn't know what preparation that the village healer created for her, but whatever it was, it smelled awful.

Darra spied the wash basin, cloth, and a silver backed looking glass that the servant left on the dressing table. Suddenly she had an urge to wash the poultice from her head.

She knew that in her container, she could find a substitute that was more pleasant to her senses. Also, consuming a willow bark preparation would help dull the throbbing in her head. Reaching into her basket, she pulled out a packet of crushed willow bark, and dropped a small amount into a cup of wine that sat at the side table.

As she drank the concoction, she drifted over to the dressing table and picked up the mirror. The woman staring back at her seemed like a haggard stranger. Her skin was sallow, and the bandage wrapped around her head made it appear large and disproportionate.

She painstakingly unwrapped the linen cloth from her head and washed away the last of the smelly poultice. Her fingers probed the tender spot and found a small bump there. She compressed her lips in disapproval. The wound was not so drastic that her head needed to be encased in such a large amount of linen. What was the village healer thinking? To see Darra's physical appearance, one would believe that she fell down a steep cliff, and bumped her head in several places.

She set aside the mirror and moved to put on her clothes, deciding to also don the *arisaid*. When she first put on the plaid, she found it complex, but now she easily folded, and belted the material around her waist. Lastly, she secured the rest of the soft fabric over her shoulder with a brooch.

Pleased with herself, she was about to adjust her belt when she heard voices in the corridor. Hurrying over to the door, she flung it open.

"Mother!" she cried.

At first, Lady Venora started at Darra's sudden appearance, and then her eyes widened when she took in Darra's attire. However, her mother recovered her senses and came over to quickly embrace her.

Darra looked past Lady Venora, and noticed that Rory, his brothers as well as Sir Dudley stood in the hallway. She turned to question her mother, but her mother only tightened her hold.

"Darra," she said, relief apparent in her voice. "I have come to take you home."

The smile faded from Darra's lips and she drew back. "But my work is not finished here, Mother," she explained. "Eanruing is still ill, and none of my remedies have worked." She didn't mention that she had her own injury to attend. But that was a detail which she didn't need to divulge.

"It does not matter," her mother said, leading her into the corridor. "The MacGregons can consult the village healer, and we will leave this place."

"The village healer was unsuccessful in healing him," she said carefully, shocked at her mother's callous disregard. "You advised me countless times that a healer must always use her God-given skills to heal the sick. Clearly Eanruing continues to be ill, and needs more assistance."

Lady Venora looked at her, conflict warring on her visage. Pain shot through her eyes, and she appeared to sway on the side of letting Eanruing die. When her mother still didn't respond, Darra glanced away. "I have learned that the Scots are people too, that they feel pain and happiness, just like we do. 'Tis the kings and queens that use the common folks as pawns. They are the ones that make us enemies of each other."

Her mother was quiet. Then she sighed. "Aye, you are right. Take me to Eanruing, and tell me what 'tis that you have done thus far."

Darra turned to Rory, silently asking for his permission. He gave the barest of nods. Grabbing her medicine basket, she led her mother, and the rest of the party down to Eanruing's bed chamber.

The elder MacGregon was sleeping fitfully in his bed, his breathing labored and heavy. She recounted all the remedies that she tried while her mother nodded her head, listening carefully to the details.

Finally, she said, "Show me the root that you used."

Darra placed the medicine basket on the side table. Sifting through her supplies, she pulled out a fresh Gaiaroot that she had dug out earlier in the day.

Lady Venora took it from her, twisted it in her hand, and frowned. She scratched the surface of the root with her fingernail and brought it to her nose to sniff. "This is not the correct root," she said.

She looked at her mother, confused. "But I am certain —"

"You are correct that this is a Gaiaroot," she interrupted. "But 'tis the Scottish kind that you have. These are not the same as the ones that grows in the lowlands." She waved the root in the air, punctuating her statement. "This Scottish variety is weak and ineffective."

Darra stared at the offending root, stunned. "That is why the fever worsened," she said, her conclusions making her stomach roil. If she continued to administer the root, Eanruing could have ultimately died.

Lady Venora nodded, and put the root back into the container. "Do not fret. There are other remedies that you have not tried. Bring me the wine."

Darra quickly grabbed the half filled cup that sat on the table.

Her mother dug through the contents of the basket, taking out the different powders and dried herbs that she needed. She carefully measured and mixed each ingredient into the wine, and swirled it around in the vessel. Dipping a finger in the mixture first, she brought it up and touched it to her tongue.

Satisfied with the formula, she took the drink to the bed.

But when her mother got to the bedside, she paused. For the longest time, she stood still, staring down at the old laird, a sad, distant look on her countenance. She seemed to be lost in some memory. Her mother had never hesitated like this before, and Darra feared that she would slip back into her misery.

Suddenly Darra recalled when Eanruing had mistaken her for Lady Venora. At that time he had apologized for something that he did to her. And then it all made sense. These two people shared an unhappy history, and it was this man that had driven her mother away from the highlands. Darra felt guilty for forcing her mother to attend to an old enemy.

But then her mother sighed. She was a healer first and foremost. Gesturing to Darra, she said, "Hold his head."

Darra went to the other side of the bed and held Eanruing while her mother forced his jaw open, and poured the medicinal liquid into his mouth. Some of the liquid dribbled at the side of his chin, but most of it was consumed.

Glancing over at Rory, her mother said, "I need you to lift him so he is in a seated position."

Rory nodded and complied with her mother's wishes.

As soon as Eanruing sat up, he began to violently sputter and cough. Shortly after color flooded into his cheeks, and he became aware of the people gathered around his bedside. His gaze shifted from Darra to Lady Venora, and then a faint spark of hope shone in his eyes.

"Venora…?" he asked faintly. He raised a weak hand as if to touch her mother's cheek.

"Aye, 'tis I," Lady Venora said, leaning away from him. "But I do not know why I saved your life."

"Aiya, will ye ever forgive me, lass?" Tears gathering at the corner of his eyes. "'Twas a misunderstanding…an accident. I dinnae mean tae kill Robart. I had a dagger, and my foot slipped and I fell…" He gulped, unable to finish. "I — I tried tae find ye, tae get your help, and stop the destruction, but I didnae ken where ye went. I couldnae stop the clan wars on my own. If I had the power tae change things, I would…"

The full weight of Eanruing's confession hung heavily in the air, and Lady Venora became silent for a long while. After a time she drew in a deep breath and released it in a rush. "I am weary of holding this wrath inside me, MacGregon," she said finally. "I am weary of hating you, of hating what you have done to me and my father. It has eaten away at my soul and killed the love and passion I have for my country and kin. But even so I have never supposed that you murdered my father. I believe what you say — that 'twas an accident." She blew out a long, shaky breath. "I forgive you. But I am not doing this to absolve you from your guilt. I am doing this to liberate myself from enmity."

"I can accept that." He nodded his head slowly while his visage twisted in painful remorse. "Thank ye."

Rory lowered his father back onto the mattress and came to stand beside Darra. He placed his arm around her shoulders and she leaned into his strength. Her mother appeared downcast, but Darra realized that she had resolved her long held grief.

Darra was glad for her, and she felt the tears prickle in her own eyes. As if Rory knew what she was thinking, he gave her shoulder a reassuring squeeze. She tilted her head to look at him and offered him a tremulous smile.

"I am sorry to break up this precious moment," Sir Dudley said sarcastically. "But the old Highlander is healed, and 'tis time for us to leave."

He sauntered over to Darra and grabbed her arm, yanking her free from Rory's embrace. Sir Dudley's fingers dug into her flesh, and she let out a cry of pain.

"Darra will nae be going anywhere with ye," Rory growled. He caught the shirtfront of Sir Dudley's tunic, forcing him to release her. Trying to get out of his grip, the older knight threw a punch at Rory's head.

Rory ducked the jab and plowed his fist into the other man's gut, causing him to double over. Gasping and sputtering, his hand reached inside his boot. When he straightened again, a dagger was in his hand and a murderous expression was on his face.

The quick movement of metal scraping across leather sounded, and Duncan held his claymore at the knight's throat.

"Stop this foolishness at once!" Lady Venora commanded. "Someone will get killed!" Her mother's sudden outburst caused everyone to pause. "I did not come here to save one man, and see another three die," she said, shaking with fury.

"Rory, please, if you care for me at all, do not let him take me," Darra said, her tone low and pleading.

He stared at her and Sir Dudley, his face in conflict. But then he shook his head. "I'm sorry lass, but ye would be safer with your own people." Inclining his head at his brother, Rory gave him silent instruction to lower his sword.

Duncan slid his weapon back into its sheath while he planted a foot on the other man's abdomen and shoved him away. Sir Dudley stumbled and when he found his footing again, he stood, furiously brushing away at the dirt on his velvet tunic.

"I dinnae want anyone tae perish," Rory said. "Eanruing is healed now." He paused and nodded to Darra, his expression unreadable. "I wish ye safe passage."

"I thought Highlanders were resilient, and willing to fight for what they wanted." Darra's countenance was devoid of blood while her blue eyes shone with unshed tears. "I see that I was wrong."

The devastated look on her beguiling face felt like an arrow piercing his gut. He averted his face, unable to meet her scrutiny. In his heart he discerned that she wasn't referring to the scuffle that occurred moments ago.

He clenched his hands, and tried to stomp down the awful, sick feeling that he was making a dreadful mistake. But he had already put Darra in danger, and she almost lost her life. The last fight involved fists. This battle involved weapons, and he couldn't risk having her, or anyone else get caught in the crossfire.

"I promised tae let ye go once Eanruing was healed," he said, "'Tis prudent that ye leave now as we dinnae want trouble."

Lady Venora looked curiously at him before taking her daughter's arm and leading her toward the chamber door. Meanwhile Dudley gave him a contemptuous sneer and followed in their wake.

Duncan came to stand beside him as they watched the trio retreat from the chamber.

"Ye did the right thing, Rory."

"Aye," he said, flatly. A muscle worked at his jaw. He accepted that he made the honorable decision by letting her go. But why did it feel so wrong?

Chapter 18

❧❧

I thought Highlanders were resilient, and willing to fight for what they wanted.

Until the day Rory died, her last words would haunt him. Darra was right however. He wanted her, but he didn't fight to keep her. She had to know that he was doing this for her benefit. If she became caught in the middle of the skirmish...he didn't even want to imagine what would happen. Darra lived a quiet life before he entered into it, and since then she had fallen into one dangerous situation after another. It was best that she went back to her home. At least then she would be safe. But even with this knowledge, it didn't make things easier to see her go.

Rory stood at the window, watching her procession move toward the gatehouse, every second taking her further and further away from him. He closed his eyes in an attempt to block out the scene. But the act only made another scene come to the forefront. He could never forget the expression on her face when he told her to leave. Her face twisted as if she fought to prevent herself from crying. This realization cut his insides, because while he tried once again to shield her from suffering, he caused more of it. He did her a favor by extracting himself from her life. It was better that she went back to England, and be with her own people. And when she married Dudley, she would be content with the creature comforts that the old knight would provide. Rory had nothing to offer that would rival the knight's wealth.

Still, the thought of Darra with another man made him miserable. *'Tis because ye are a damn fool*, a voice inside his head insisted. *Ye shouldnae have let her go.*

"Rory?" Mairead's soft voice said, interrupting his thoughts.

He looked over at his sister, and saw the concern and worry on her visage. He smiled at her to put her at ease, although he didn't really feel like smiling. She walked closer to him. "I offered for them tae stay here until first light, but Darr — *Lady* Darra," Mairead corrected herself, "said that she wanted tae leave immediately…"

"Aye," he said. "I can see that."

Mairead stood at his side as if she was uncertain what else to say. Likely she had never seen him in this state. He was not one to wallow in his melancholy, but right now his heart felt weighted, as if a boulder crushed down upon it.

She touched his arm, sympathy etched on her youthful countenance. Her demeanor was so much like their mother's. "Do ye want me tae bring ye something?" she asked.

"Go on with your duties," he said gruffly, "I'll be fine."

"All right," she said, unable to conceal the doubt in her voice. "But if ye need me, I'll be in the great hall going over the accounts with the steward."

He nodded and went back to survey the courtyard. The last of Darra's troop had disappeared, and the loss became absolute. He pushed away from the window, no longer wanting to stare at the emptiness.

"What is wrong with ye, lad?" Eanruing said from his bed. Since Lady Venora had administered the medication, the fever had left him, and he seemed more vigorous and alert. He shifted in his bed and sat up so that he could get a better look at Rory. "It appears tae me that ye are sulking."

"'Tis because he's in love," Duncan said from the other side of the room.

His brother's statement jolted him. Were his feelings that transparent?

The rest of his siblings had gone off to their chores, but he forgot that Duncan remained in the chamber with him and his father.

"Love," his father said, rolling the word slowly in his mouth.

"Aye," Duncan said. He was seated and drinking spiced wine, but now he got up. "I think I've change my mind about what I said about ye doing the right thing." He tipped the cup to his lips and drained the last of its contents. "Ye need tae go after the lass."

"I thought ye hated her," Rory said, unable to keep the surprise from his voice.

"Aiya, hate is a word that is a wee bit strong," Duncan said, wincing. "In any case, I have been known tae be wrong on occasion." He put his cup aside and walked over to him. "If ye let her go, ye will become an embittered, unbearable arse. Who can live with that? Nae me. Do yourself and everyone else a favor, and go claim your lass. 'Tis obvious that she loves ye too."

He was about to argue with him when Eanruing joined in. "He's right, ye ken."

Rory twisted to see his father, shocked that he would side with Duncan. Eanruing stared, his expression grave and sorrowful.

"If ye really love the lass, then ye owe it tae yourself tae go after her," his father continued slowly. "Dinnae repeat history, and make the same mistake I did. If ye do, ye will surely regret it." He set his head back down on his pillow. "Now go!"

**

"Riders follow us," Sir Jarin said.

The sound was faint at first, but there was no mistaking the steady thud of horse hooves drumming in the distance. Both her mother and Darra stopped their horses and looked behind them.

"Who can it be?" Lady Venora said, squinting.

The leading horseman was crouched low on his horse, moving at a breakneck speed. Two other riders rode behind him.

Darra nudged the horse with her knees to wheel the horse around and urge it forward. "'Tis none of our concern," she murmured.

She was past caring. Any feelings she had were trampled by Rory MacGregon. She had given him her body and her heart, although it was obvious that he didn't want either. At the moment she just wanted to get back to Lancullin Castle. She would join her mother in working with the sick, and in time, Rory would become a faded memory.

Out of the corner of her eye, she saw Sir Dudley riding beside her. Darra recognized that he still had intentions of marrying her. He had spoken at length about how her life would improve once she became his wife. On a couple of occasions, she caught her mother's sympathetic glance. But Darra's dilemma gnawed at her gut. How was she to reveal to him that she was no longer a virgin? Or that she would rather cross a pack of feral dogs than be wed to him?

The sound of pounding hooves came closer and closer until they were upon them.

"Darra!" a voice shouted.

Her heart froze; she would never be able to forget that deep voice. But she allowed her horse to continue forward. Likely if she turned around, she would melt under the influence of his devastating charms.

"Darra, wait!"

"Would you like to stop, milady?" Sir Jarin asked Darra.

When she hesitated, her mother spoke up. "Let us find out what the MacGregon wants."

Sir Jarin nodded and then raised his hand in the air. "Halt!"

"We have a distance to cover, and should not be stopping," Sir Dudley said, irritation in his voice. He started to move forward with his men, but the Lancullin guards stayed where they were.

"What do you want with my daughter, Rory MacGregon?" her mother said when Rory was within earshot. "I believe your father is healed, and our work is finished here."

"Nay, not finished, milady. I desire tae speak with Lady Darra."

The rest of the MacGregon siblings rode in, stopping their horses beside their brother's.

"Whatever you have to say can be said for all to hear," Darra said, although she averted her face, still not trusting herself to look at him. Knowing that he was close by caused her heart to beat uncontrollably. But then she couldn't help it any longer, and she peered over at him. As soon as she saw his comely face, the air sucked out from her lungs. His red hair was windswept, and he appeared as wild as the highlands. It was absolutely sinful how a man could be so powerful and vulnerable at the same time. She felt a stabbing pain in her heart and she turned away again.

Rory maneuvered his horse until he was in front of her. "Darra."

Though she didn't want to, she raised her eyes and gazed into his green depths. A jolt went through her body, and the energy of it left her flushed.

"I love ye," he said, not caring that others heard him. His eyes were trained on her and nothing else. He jumped off his horse and came to her. Taking her hand, he laid it on his cheek. "With each day I've come tae ken ye, ye proved more and more precious tae me. I was a fool tae let ye go, lass, wrong tae even suggest ye leave. I have never liked weak lassies." He swallowed and searched her face. "And from the moment I caught sight of ye, I found ye tae be strong and brave. The memory of ye, a wee lass, brandishing a large broadsword still brings a smile tae my face. And your melodic voice. It echoes in my mind, and haunts my sleep." His emerald eyes glittered as emotion flowed into his voice. "I dinnae think I can live without ye, lass. Say that ye will stay here — with me. Say that ye will be my wife."

She opened her mouth, but no sound came out. All she could do was stare at Rory. In fact everyone in the troop gaped at him in stunned silence. This was a large and menacing Highland Chief who was capable of causing grievous damage to anyone who crossed him. Yet here he was, pouring his heart out to her, telling her that he adored her.

Tears streamed down her cheeks. "I —"

"What nonsense is this?" Sir Dudley demanded. Then his voice turned icy. "Lady Darra is marrying *me*, not you. Step away from her, and crawl back to the hell hole from which you were born."

He pulled his broadsword from his scabbard and moved his horse closer to Darra. Hatred spewed from his small eyes, and if Rory's brothers were not at his back, he would have run Rory through with his sword.

"Ye ask the impossible," Rory said, reaching casually behind him and withdrawing his claymore from its sheath. "The lass is mine."

"She does not belong to you —"

"Aye, she does," he said, leveling his gaze on the other man, making his meaning clear. "And I belong tae her."

Sir Dudley's eyes bulged at Rory's implied words.

"Ye see," Rory continued, "A Highlander *is* resilient, and always fights for what he wants. But he also has the support of his clan," he said, glancing over his shoulder.

Sir Dudley jerked back and saw the truth in what Rory said. While he spoke, he failed to notice that more than a dozen of Rory's clan members were arriving, a trail of dust following them as they thundered closer. Soon enough the men halted and surrounded the entourage. Every single MacGregon appeared merciless and menacing; their weapons were drawn and ready to attack at Rory's command.

"Ye can stay and fight, but if ye choose tae do sae, I'll wager that ye willnae leave Scotland alive." Rory stared intently at the older knight. "However if ye relinquish your claim on Lady Darra, and leave peacefully, my men will let ye pass. 'Tis your choice."

Sir Dudley sat on his horse, his face purple with rage. He looked over at her, a moment of indecision reflected on his features. He couldn't know if Rory was bluffing about their relations. And if he married Darra, and she became pregnant, he bore the risk that the child she carried might not be his.

The knight's lips curled into a sneer. "You can have her," he said, shoving his sword forcefully back into its scabbard. "No whore is worth dying for."

"Have a care, sire," Rory's grip on his sword tightened. "I may yet change my mind, and kill ye for your insult."

"Men!" he snarled, and kicked his horse into action.

The Highlanders parted to allow him and his small troop to pass. As Darra watched the knight and his men disappear, the tension released from her shoulders. She was finally free from Sir Dudley. Turning back to Rory, she was about to make a comment when she discovered him watching her.

"Ye still havenae answered my question, lass. Will ye marry me?"

"Aye," her face softened, and she bent down and placed a hand on his cheek. "I will marry you."

A grin appeared on his rugged countenance, and he threw back his head and let out a loud whoop. Reaching up, he pulled her down from the horse.

"I love you, Rory MacGregon," she said, lightly caressing his jaw. "I have loved you for a long time now."

"I'm glad," he said. Then bending his head, he gave her a soul-shattering kiss while his clan members lustily hollered and cheered them on.

When the noise dwindled, her mother maneuvered her horse closer to them, and delicately cleared her throat. "Is this what you really want, Darra — to stay here?"

Darra glanced over at her mother. She knew instinctively that if she gave any sign that she desired to vacate this place, her mother would assist her. But Darra already made her decision.

"Aye, mother, I am staying here." And then looking up at Rory with love warming her heart, she said, "For the highlands is where I belong."

To My Readers...

Thank you for purchasing this book. If you enjoyed this story, I would be most grateful if you would take a few seconds to write a review for it, and to spread the word about it to your friends.

Many thanks,
Dana D'Angelo

P.S. To keep up-to-date with the latest news, upcoming releases, and members-only specials, please sign up for my newsletter at

http://www.dana-dangelo.com/bookshelf.php

About The Author

Dana D'Angelo is the only girl from a family of nine children. As a teenager, there was a constant battle for the T.V. remote, which she lost, so she was forced to find her amusement in books. A friend got her into romances, and soon she read as many as ten romance novels per week, spending hours with her nose pressed between the pages, skipping meals and cutting out sleep. Life, it seemed, wasn't as exciting or interesting as in the Medieval or Regency eras.

It wasn't until she was married with two young kids that she decided to take a stab at writing her own historical romance novels.

She is intrigued with the idea of writing romantic stories that could bring hours of enjoyment to readers, help them escape from reality, and perhaps remind them how sweet love is and should be. These are the things that she enjoys as a reader, and these are the things that she wants to give back as a writer.

Dana lives in a city east of Toronto, Canada. When she's not writing or reading, she's dining at local restaurants with her husband and kids and enjoying spectacular foods of the world.

Website: www.dana-dangelo.com

Glossary

Some words I used in this story are not commonly used in standard English, so for those interested, I've compiled a short list of the terms and their meanings.

Aiya — Ouch

Arisaid — Scottish woman's dress similar to a Highlander's great kilt

Blether — Babble, talk nonsense

Braw — beautiful, fine, or handsome

Claymore — A double-edged sword that Highlanders used

Leine — Undershirt worn underneath a kilt or kirtle

Michaelmas — Feast of St. Michael the Archangel which is celebrated on September 29th of each year

Och — Oh

Sassenach — An English person, or a Lowland Scot

Shellycoat — A bogeyman who haunts the Scottish rivers and streams. He's said to wear a coat of shells which rattle when he moves

Sporran — A pouch or purse worn around the waist, and hangs at the front of the kilt

Tanist — Usually elected, this person is the next in line to become chief

Bruce County Public Library
1243 Mackenzie Rd.
Port Elgin ON N0H 2C6

CPSIA information can be obtained at www.ICGtesting.com
Printed in the USA
LVOW11s2042250216

476707LV00001B/23/P